THE BOLD DRAGOON

And Other Ghostly Tales

Here are five of Irving's best mystery stories, ranging from the riotous night spent by the bold dragoon in the Haunted Chamber of the old inn at Bruges, to the search for the coveted treasure of Kidd the Pirate along the American coast.

Edited with painstaking care by Anne Carroll Moore, the tales retain all their essential drama, satire, and sensitiveness to beauty, and James Daugherty's pictures of the Dutch citizens, old Manhattan, and the supernatural have all the humor and imagination of Washington Irving himself.

MY GRANDFATHER

The BOLD DRAGOON

And other ghostly tales
by WASHINGTON
IRVING

selected and edited
by
ANNE CARROLL MOORE
with
decorative diversions by
JAMES DAUGHERTY

and pleasingly published
by ALFRED·A·KNOPF·
new · AMSTERDAM

Published August 1930
Fifteenth Printing, January 1967

THIS IS A BORZOI BOOK,
PUBLISHED BY ALFRED A. KNOPF, INC.

MANUFACTURED IN THE UNITED STATES OF AMERICA

CONTENTS

To the memory of ANNA COGSWELL TYLER *and the* BOYS AND GIRLS OF NEW YORK *with whom she shared a true storyteller's love of the mystery and adventure in these tales.*

INTRODUCTION

It was a glorious October day, close upon Hallowe'en. I had made my annual pilgrimage up through Sleepy Hollow and the spell of that lovely region was upon me more strongly than ever as I climbed to the top of the Aqueduct and strolled on, thinking of Washington Irving and his marvellous power of evoking the supernatural while recording the purely natural aspects of the Hudson River country.

The sun dropped down behind his Fairy Mountains, flooding the river with purple and gold, and the silver crescent of a new moon appeared in the sky. There was no one in sight. One felt very remote up there at twilight, very far away from mountains of skyscrapers, very near to the fair island of Manahatta with its great tulip and chestnut trees and its densely wooded, mystery haunted shores.

Believe it or not, it is still possible to recapture in that setting the thrill one felt on first listening to the tale of the Headless Horseman and his ghostly pursuit of poor Ichabod Crane through the Hollow. As I walked on down the Aqueduct toward Tarrytown the sense of mystery, of wonder, of beauty remained with me. The spirit of place was mine for that hour, the imperishable gift of Washington Irving.

The whole world had changed in a single afternoon. I entered the subway refreshed and restored, my mind began to work on a new idea. In an age so eager for good mystery stories, why leave Washington Irving's in cold storage? Since I was alone I put the question to myself.

Where could one look for a more hair-raising story than Tom Walker's encounter with the Devil, where for one that haunts the memory like the Storm Ship in Dolph Heyliger, or one more gruesome than the Guests from Gibbet Island who visited the Blue Chamber of the inn at Communipaw? Where is to be found more prophetic insight into the real estate development of our City than among the " golden dreams " of Wolfert Webber? Mystery stories, every one of them, with an authentic background of our own beloved coast in the time of Kidd the Pirate.

Boys like the stories individually, why should they not like them collectively? Girls too, I can think of any number who would. Why shouldn't the impoverished adults who have never read Irving for fun but merely as required reading in school have the time of their lives with such tales as these. Ghostly tales they truly are, and a jolly one to add from overseas is The Bold Dragoon who spent a riotous night in the Haunted Chamber of an old inn at Bruges. James Daugherty will know just how the Bold Dragoon ought to look, I reflected, and Dolph Heyliger, a boy after his own heart, and the Storm Ship, and the Money Diggers, one and all, from Corlaer's Hook on the East River, up Long Island Sound to Boston-on-the-Charles. James Daugherty must certainly lend a hand to the making of the book.

This, in brief, is the story of the origin of The Bold Dragoon and Other Ghostly Tales. Born in the murk and roar of an on-rushing subway train, it found an understanding publisher that very night. The text has been cut to some extent but only for its digressions. In no instance has the essential drama of a story been touched. The editing, in short, has proceeded on the plan of preparing a story to be read aloud by freeing it from sentences and paragraphs which impede its progress as a story. Such descriptive passages as give colour and authenticity to the background have been retained. Dolph Heyliger, for example, contains some of Irving's best descriptive writing and one must chart one's editorial course with full regard for the Hudson River, Albany, and all other historic points as well as for Dolph's personal adventures.

The more I read and reread the writings of Washington Irving the more certain I feel that he belongs outside of school reading books. He was not in the least academic. He left school behind at an early age and abandoned the profession of law. He was a traveller with an international mind, a free spirit imbued with an intense love of his own country born of his exploration of the beauty, the mystery, and the human affairs of the Hudson River and the little old New York of his boyhood. We need Irving today. We need his tolerance, his kindliness, the tonic of his satire, his sensitiveness to beauty, and above all do we need his ready belief in the goblins and great men of the countries through which he travelled in actuality and in imagination. ANNE CARROLL MOORE

The High Tower
East River
May 15, 1930

THE BOLD DRAGOON

The Bold Dragoon

MY GRANDFATHER was a bold dragoon, for it's a profession, d' ye see, that has run in the family. All my forefathers have been dragoons, and died on the field of honor, except myself, and I hope my posterity may be able to say the same; however, I don't mean to be vainglorious. Well, my grandfather, as I said, was a bold dragoon, and had served in the Low Countries. In fact, he was one of that very army, which according to my uncle Toby, swore so terribly in Flanders. He could swear a good stick himself; and moreover was the very man that introduced the doctrine Corporal Trim mentions of radical heat and radical moisture, or, in other words, the mode of keeping out the damps of ditchwater by burnt brandy. My grandfather was a man not easily to be humbugged. He had

3

seen service, or, according to his own phrase, he had seen the devil — and that's saying everything.

Well, gentlemen, my grandfather was on his way to England, for which he intended to embark from Ostend. So one evening, towards night fall, he rode jollily into Bruges. — Very like you all know Bruges, gentlemen; a queer, old-fashioned Flemish town, once, they say, a great place for trade and money-making in old times, when the Mynheers were in their glory; but almost as large and as empty as an Irishman's pocket at the present day. — Well, gentlemen, it was at the time of the annual fair. All Bruges was crowded; and the canals swarmed with Dutch boats, and the streets swarmed with Dutch merchants; and there was hardly any getting along for goods, wares, and merchandises, and peasants in big breeches, and women in half a score of petticoats.

My grandfather rode jollily along, in his easy, slashing way, for he was a saucy, sunshiny fellow — staring about him at the motley crowd, the old houses with gable ends to the street, and storks' nests in the chimneys; winking at the yafrows who showed their faces at the windows and joking the women right and left in the street; all of whom laughed, and took it in amazing good part; for though he did not know a word of the language, yet he had always a knack of making himself understood among the women.

Well, gentlemen, it being the time of the annual fair, all the town was crowded, every inn and tavern full, and my grandfather applied in vain from one to the other for admittance. At length he rode up to an old rickety inn, that looked ready to

4

fall to pieces, and which all the rats would have run away from, if they could have found room in any other house to put their heads. It was just such a queer building as you see in Dutch pictures, with a tall roof that reached up into the clouds, and as many garrets, one over the other, as the seven heavens of Mahomet. Nothing had saved it from tumbling down but a stork's nest on the chimney, which always brings good luck to a house in the Low Countries; and at the very time of my grandfather's arrival, there were two of these long-legged birds of grace standing like ghosts on the chimney-top.

My grandfather eyed the house curiously as he approached. It might not have altogether struck his fancy, had he not seen in large letters over the door,

HEER VERKOOPT MAN GOEDEN DRANK.

My grandfather had learnt enough of the language to know that the sign promised good liquor. " This is the house for me," said he, stopping short before the door.

The sudden appearance of a dashing dragoon was an event in an old inn frequented only by the peaceful sons of traffic. A rich burgher of Antwerp, a stately ample man in a broad Flemish hat, and who was the great man and great patron of the establishment, sat smoking a clean long pipe on one side of the door; a fat little distiller of Geneva, from Schiedam, sat smoking on the other; and the bottle-nosed host stood in the door, and the comely hostess, in crimped cap, beside him; and the hostess's daughter, a plump Flanders lass, with long gold pendants in her ears, was at a side-window.

"Humph!" said the rich burgher of Antwerp, with a sulky glance at the stranger.

"De duyvel!" said the fat little distiller of Schiedam.

The landlord saw, with the quick glance of a publican, that the new guest was not at all to the taste of the old ones; and, to tell the truth, he did not like my grandfather's saucy eye. He shook his head. "Not a garret in the house but was full."

"Not a garret!" echoed the landlady.

"Not a garret!" echoed the daughter.

The burgher of Antwerp, and the little distiller of Schiedam, continued to smoke their pipes sullenly, eying the enemy askance from under their broad hats, but said nothing.

My grandfather was not a man to be browbeaten. He threw the reins on his horse's neck, cocked his head on one side, stuck

6

one arm akimbo, — " Faith and troth! " said he, " but I'll sleep in this house this very night." — As he said this he gave a slap on his thigh, by way of emphasis — the slap went to the landlady's heart.

He followed up the vow by jumping off his horse, and making his way past the staring Mynheers into the public room. — Maybe you've been in the bar-room of an old Flemish inn — faith, but a handsome chamber it was as you'd wish to see; with a brick floor, and a great fireplace, with the whole Bible history in glazed tiles; and then the mantel-piece, pitching itself head foremost out of the wall, with a whole regiment of cracked tea-pots and earthen jugs paraded on it; not to mention half a dozen great Delft platters, hung about the room by way of pictures; and the little bar in one corner, and the bouncing bar-maid inside of it, with a red calico cap, and yellow ear-drops.

My grandfather snapped his fingers over his head, as he cast an eye round the room, — " Faith, this is the very house I've been looking after," said he.

There was some further show of resistance on the part of the garrison; but my grandfather was an old soldier, and an Irishman to boot, and not easily repulsed, especially after he had got into the fortress. So he blarneyed the landlord, kissed the landlord's wife, tickled the landlord's daughter, chucked the bar-maid under the chin; and it was agreed on all hands that it would be a thousand pities, and a burning shame into the bargain, to turn such a bold dragoon into the streets. So they laid their heads together, that is to say, my grandfather and the

7

landlady, and it was at length agreed to accommodate him with an old chamber that had been for some time shut up.

"Some say it's haunted," whispered the landlord's daughter; "but you are a bold dragoon, and I dare say don't fear ghosts."

"The devil a bit!" said my grandfather, pinching her plump cheek. "But if I should be troubled by ghosts, I've been to the Red Sea in my time, and have a pleasant way of laying them, my darling."

And then he whispered something to the girl which made her laugh, and give him a good-humoured box on the ear. In short, there was nobody knew better how to make his way among the petticoats than my grandfather.

In a little while, as was his usual way, he took complete possession of the house, swaggering all over it; into the stable to look after his horse, into the kitchen to look after his supper. He had something to say or do with everyone; smoked with the Dutchmen, drank with the Germans, slapped the landlord on the shoulder, romped with his daughter and the bar-maid: — never, since the days of Alley Croaker, had such a rattling blade been seen. The landlord stared at him with astonishment; the landlord's daughter hung her head and giggled whenever he came near; and as he swaggered along the corridor, with his sword trailing by his side, the maids looked after him, and whispered to one another, "What a proper man!"

At supper, my grandfather took command of the *table-d'hôte* as though he had been at home; helped everybody, not forgetting himself; talked with every one, whether he understood

8

their language or not; and made his way into the intimacy of the rich burgher of Antwerp, who had never been known to be sociable with any one during his life. In fact, he revolutionized the whole establishment, and gave it such a rouse, that the very house reeled with it. He outsat everyone at table, excepting the little fat distiller of Schiedam, who sat soaking a long time before he broke forth; but when he did, he was a very devil incarnate. He took a violent affection for my grandfather; so they sat drinking and smoking, and telling stories, and singing Dutch and Irish songs, without understanding a word each other said, until the little Hollander was fairly swamped with his own gin and water, and carried off to bed, whooping and hiccuping, and trolling the burden of a Low Dutch love-song.

Well, gentlemen, my grandfather was shown to his quarters up a large staircase, composed of loads of hewn timber; and through long rigmarole passages, hung with blackened paintings of fish, and fruit, and game, and country frolics, and huge kitchens, and portly burgomasters, such as you see about old-fashioned Flemish inns, till at length he arrived at his room.

An old-times chamber it was, sure enough, and crowded with all kinds of trumpery. It looked like an infirmary for decayed and superannuated furniture, where everything diseased or disabled was sent to nurse or to be forgotten. No two chairs were alike. Such high backs and low backs, and leather bottoms, and worsted bottoms, and straw bottoms, and no bottoms; and cracked marble tables with curiously carved legs, holding balls in their claws, as though they were going to play at ninepins.

My grandfather made a bow to the motley assemblage as he

THE TAVERN AT BRUGES

entered, and, having undressed himself, placed his light in the fireplace, asking pardon of the tongs, which seemed to be making love to the shovel in the chimney-corner, and whispering soft nonsense in its ear.

The rest of the guests were by this time sound asleep, for your Mynheers are huge sleepers. The housemaids, one by one, crept up yawning to their attics; and not a female head in the inn was laid on a pillow that night without dreaming of the bold dragoon.

My grandfather, for his part, got into bed, and drew over him one of those great bags of down, under which they smother a man in the Low Countries; and there he lay, melting between two feather beds, like an anchovy sandwich between two slices of toast and butter. He was a warm-complexioned man, and this smothering played the very deuce with him. So, sure enough, in a little time it seemed as if a legion of imps were twitching at him, and all the blood in his veins was in a fever-heat.

He lay still, however, until all the house was quiet excepting the snoring of the Mynheers from the different chambers; who answered one another in all kinds of tones and cadences, like so many bull-frogs in a swamp. My grandfather waxed warmer and warmer, until at length the bed became too hot to hold him.

"Faith, there's no standing this any longer," says he. So he jumped out of bed, and went strolling about the house.

Well, my grandfather had been for some time absent from his room, and was returning, perfectly cool, when just as he reached the door, he heard a strange noise within. He paused

·THE·HAUNTED·BEDCHAMBER·

and listened. It seemed as if some one were trying to hum a tune in defiance of the asthma. He recollected the report of the room being haunted; but he was no believer in ghosts, so he pushed the door gently open and peeped in.

Egad, gentlemen, there was a gambol carrying on within enough to have astonished St. Anthony himself. By the light of the fire he saw a pale weazen-faced fellow, in a long flannel gown and a tall white night-cap with a tassel to it, who sat by the fire with a bellows under his arm by way of bagpipe, from which he forced the asthmatical music that had bothered my grandfather. As he played, too, he kept twitching about with a thousand queer contortions, nodding his head, and bobbing about his tasselled night-cap.

My grandfather thought this very odd and mighty presumptuous, and was about to demand what business he had to play his wind-instrument in another gentleman's quarters, when a new cause of astonishment met his eye. From the opposite side of the room a long-backed, bandy-legged chair, covered with leather, and studded all over in a coxcombical fashion with little brass nails, got suddenly into motion, thrust out first a claw-foot, then a crooked arm, and at length, making a leg, slided gracefully up to an easy-chair of tarnished brocade, with a hole in its bottom, and led it gallantly out in a ghostly minuet about the floor.

The musician now played fiercer and fiercer, and bobbed his head and his night-cap about like mad. By degrees the dancing mania seemed to seize upon all the other pieces of furniture. The antique, long-bodied chairs paired off in couples and led

14

down a country-dance; a three-legged stool danced a hornpipe, though horribly puzzled by its supernumerary limb; while the amorous tongs seized the shovel round the waist, and whirled it about the room in a German waltz. In short, all the movables got in motion; pirouetting hands across, right and left, like so many devils; all except a great clothes-press, which kept courtesying and courtesying in a corner, like a dowager, in exquisite time to the music; being rather too corpulent to dance, or perhaps at a loss for a partner.

My grandfather concluded the latter to be the reason; so being, like a true Irishman, devoted to the sex, and at all times ready for a frolic, he bounced into the room, called to the musician to strike up Paddy O'Rafferty, capered up to the clothes-press, and seized upon the two handles to lead her out:——— when whirr! the whole revel was at an end. The chairs, tables, tongs and shovel, slunk in an instant as quietly into their places as if nothing had happened, and the musician vanished up the

chimney, leaving the bellows behind him in his hurry. My grandfather found himself seated in the middle of the floor with the clothes-press sprawling before him, and the two handles jerked off, and in his hands.

Well, gentlemen, as the clothes-press was a mighty heavy body, and my grandfather likewise, particularly in rear, you may easily suppose that two such heavy bodies coming to the ground would make a bit of a noise. Faith, the old mansion shook as though it had mistaken it for an earthquake. The whole garrison was alarmed. The landlord, who slept below, hurried up with a candle to inquire the cause, but with all his haste his daughter had arrived at the scene of uproar before him. The landlord was followed by the landlady, who was followed by the bouncing bar-maid, who was followed by the simpering chambermaids, all holding together, as well as they could, such garments as they first laid hands on; but all in a terrible hurry to see what the deuce was to pay in the chamber of the bold dragoon.

17

My grandfather related the marvellous scene he had witnessed, and the broken handles of the prostrate clothes-press bore testimony to the fact. There was no contesting such evidence; particularly with a lad of my grandfather's complexion, who seemed able to make good every word either with sword or shillelah. So the landlord scratched his head and looked silly, as he was apt to do when puzzled. The landlady scratched — no, she did not scratch her head, but she knit her brow, and did not seem half pleased with the explanation. But the landlady's daughter corroborated it by recollecting that the last person who had dwelt in that chamber was a famous juggler who died of St. Vitus's dance, and had no doubt infected all the furniture.

This set all things to rights, particularly when the chambermaids declared that they had all witnessed strange carryings on in that room; and as they declared this " upon their honors," there could not remain a doubt upon this subject.

THE DEVIL AND TOM WALKER

. KIDD THE PIRATE .

The Devil and Tom Walker

A FEW MILES from Boston in Massachusetts, there is a deep inlet, winding several miles into the interior of the country from Charles Bay, and terminating in a thickly-wooded swamp or morass. On one side of this inlet is a beautiful dark grove; on the opposite side the land rises abruptly from the water's edge into a high ridge, on which grow a few scattered oaks of great age and immense size. Under one of these gigantic trees, according to old stories, there was a great amount of treasure buried by Kidd the pirate. The inlet allowed a facility to bring the money in a boat secretly and at night to the very foot of the hill; the elevation of the place permitted a good lookout to be kept that no one was at hand; while the remarkable trees formed good landmarks by which the place might easily be found again. The old stories add, moreover, that the devil presided at the hiding of the money, and took it under his guardianship; but this, it is well known, he always does with buried treasure, particularly when it has been ill-gotten. Be that as it may, Kidd never returned to recover his wealth; being shortly after seized at Boston, sent out to England, and there hanged for a pirate.

About the year 1727, just at the time that earthquakes were prevalent in New England, and shook many tall sinners down upon their knees, there lived near this place a meagre, miserly

23

fellow, of the name of Tom Walker. He had a wife as miserly as himself: they were so miserly that they even conspired to cheat each other. Whatever the woman could lay hands on, she hid away; a hen could not cackle but she was on the alert to secure the new-laid egg. Her husband was continually prying about to detect her secret hoards, and many and fierce were the conflicts that took place about what ought to have been common property. They lived in a forlorn-looking house that stood alone, and had an air of starvation. A few straggling savin-trees, emblems of sterility, grew near it; no smoke ever curled from its chimney; no traveller stopped at its door. A miserable horse, whose ribs were as articulate as the bars of a gridiron, stalked about a field, where a thin carpet of moss, scarcely covering the ragged beds of pudding-stone, tantalized and balked his hunger; and sometimes he would lean his head over the fence, look piteously at the passer-by, and seem to petition deliverance from this land of famine.

The house and its inmates had altogether a bad name. Tom's wife was a tall termagant, fierce of temper, loud of

tongue, and strong of arm. Her voice was often heard in wordy warfare with her husband; and his face sometimes showed signs that their conflicts were not confined to words. No one ventured, however, to interfere between them. The lonely wayfarer shrunk within himself at the horrid clamor and clapper-clawing; eyed the den of discord askance; and hurried on his way, rejoicing, if a bachelor, in his celibacy.

One day that Tom Walker had been to a distant part of the neighborhood, he took what he considered a short cut homeward, through the swamp. Like most short cuts, it was an ill-chosen route. The swamp was thickly grown with great gloomy pines and hemlocks, some of them ninety feet high, which made it dark at noonday, and a retreat for all the owls of the neighborhood. It was full of pits and quagmires, partly covered with weeds and mosses, where the green surface often betrayed the traveller into a gulf of black, smothering mud; there were also dark and stagnant pools, the abodes of the tadpole, the bull-frog, and the water-snake; where the trunks of pines and hemlocks lay half drowned, half rotting, looking like alligators sleeping in the mire.

Tom had long been picking his way cautiously through this treacherous forest; stepping from tuft to tuft of rushes and roots, which afforded precarious footholds among deep sloughs; or pacing carefully, like a cat, along the prostrate trunks of trees; startled now and then by the sudden screaming of the bittern, or the quacking of wild duck rising on the wing from some solitary pool. At length he arrived at a firm piece of ground, which ran out like a peninsula into the deep bosom of

26

DISCORD

the swamp. It had been one of the strongholds of the Indians during their wars with the first colonists. Here they had thrown up a kind of fort, which they had looked upon as almost impregnable, and had used as a place of refuge for their squaws and children. Nothing remained of the old Indian fort but a few embankments, gradually sinking to the level of the surrounding earth, and already overgrown in part by oaks and other forest trees, the foliage of which formed a contrast to the dark pines and hemlocks of the swamp.

It was late in the dusk of evening when Tom Walker reached the old fort, and he paused there awhile to rest himself. Any one but he would have felt unwilling to linger in this lonely, melancholy place, for the common people had a bad opinion of it, from the stories handed down from the time of the Indian wars; when it was asserted that the savages held incantations here, and made sacrifices to the evil spirit.

Tom Walker was not a man to be troubled with any fears of the kind. He reposed himself for some time on the trunk of a fallen hemlock, listening to the boding cry of the tree-toad, and delving with his walking-staff into a mound of black mould at his feet. As he turned up the soil unconsciously, his staff struck against something hard. He raked it out of the vegetable mould, and lo! a cloven skull, with an Indian tomahawk buried deep in it, lay before him. The rust on the weapon showed the time that had elapsed since this death-blow had been given. It was a dreary memento of the fierce struggle that had taken place in this last foothold of the Indian warriors.

"Humph!" said Tom Walker, as he gave it a kick to shake the dirt from it.

"Let that skull alone!" said a gruff voice. Tom lifted up his eyes, and beheld a great black man seated directly opposite him, on the stump of a tree. He was exceedingly surprised, having neither heard nor seen any one approach; and he was still more perplexed on observing, as well as the gathering gloom would permit, that the stranger was neither negro nor Indian. It is true he was dressed in a rude half Indian garb, and had a red belt or sash swathed round his body; but his face was neither black nor copper-color, but swarthy and dingy, and begrimed with soot, as if he had been accustomed to toil among fires and forges. He had a shock of coarse black hair, that stood out from his head in all directions, and bore an axe on his shoulder.

He scowled for a moment at Tom with a pair of great red eyes.

"What are you doing on my grounds?" said the black man, with a hoarse, growling voice.

"Your grounds!" said Tom, with a sneer, "no more your grounds than mine; they belong to Deacon Peabody."

"Deacon Peabody be d——d," said the stranger, "as I flatter myself he will be, if he does not look more to his own sins and less to those of his neighbors. Look yonder, and see how Deacon Peabody is faring."

Tom looked in the direction that the stranger pointed, and beheld one of the great trees, fair and flourishing without, but rotten at the core, and saw that it had been nearly hewn through,

30

so that the first high wind was likely to blow it down. On the bark of the tree was scored the name of Deacon Peabody, an eminent man, who had waxed wealthy by driving shrewd bargains with the Indians. He now looked around, and found most of the tall trees marked with the name of some great man of the colony, and all more or less scored by the axe. The one on which he had been seated, and which had evidently just been hewn down, bore the name of Crowninshield; and he recollected a mighty rich man of that name, who made a vulgar display of wealth, which it was whispered he had acquired by buccaneering.

" He's just ready for burning! " said the black man, with a growl of triumph. " You see I am likely to have a good stock of firewood for winter."

" But what right have you," said Tom, " to cut down Deacon Peabody's timber? "

" The right of a prior claim," said the other. " This woodland belonged to me long before one of your white-faced race put foot upon the soil."

" And pray, who are you, if I may be so bold? " said Tom.

" Oh, I go by various names. I am the wild huntsman in some countries; the black miner in others. In this neighborhood I am known by the name of the black woodsman. I am he to whom the red men consecrated this spot, and in honor of whom they now and then roasted a white man, by way of sweet-smelling sacrifice. Since the red men have been exterminated by you white savages, I amuse myself by presiding at the

31

persecutions of Quakers and Anabaptists; I am the great patron and prompter of slave-dealers, and the grand-master of the Salem witches."

" The upshot of all which is, that, if I mistake not," said Tom, sturdily, " you are he commonly called Old Scratch."

" The same, at your service! " replied the black man, with a half civil nod.

One would think that to meet with such a singular personage, in this wild, lonely place, would have shaken any man's nerves; but Tom was a hard-minded fellow, not easily daunted, and he had lived so long with a termagant wife, that he did not even fear the devil.

It is said that after this commencement they had a long and earnest conversation together, as Tom returned homeward. The black man told him of great sums of money buried by Kidd the pirate, under the oak-trees on the high ridge, not far from the morass. All these were under his command, and protected by his power, so that none could find them but such as propitiated his favor. These he offered to place within Tom Walker's reach, having conceived an especial kindness for him; but they were to be had only on certain conditions. What these conditions were may be easily surmised, though Tom never disclosed them publicly. They must have been very hard, for he required time to think of them, and he was not a man to stick at trifles when money was in view. When they had reached the edge of the swamp, the stranger paused. " What proof have I that all you have been telling me is true? " said Tom. " There's my

signature," said the black man, pressing his finger on Tom's forehead. So saying, he turned off among the thickest of the swamp, and seemed, as Tom said, to go down, down, down, into the earth, until nothing but his head and shoulders could be seen, and so on, until he totally disappeared.

When Tom reached home, he found the black print of a finger burnt, as it were, into his forehead, which nothing could obliterate.

The first news his wife had to tell him was the sudden death of Absalom Crowninshield, the rich buccaneer. It was announced in the papers with the usual flourish, that " A great man had fallen in Israel."

Tom recollected the tree which his black friend had just hewn down, and which was ready for burning. " Let the freebooter roast," said Tom; " who cares! " He now felt convinced that all he had heard and seen was no illusion.

He was not prone to let his wife into his confidence; but as this was an uneasy secret, he willingly shared it with her. All her avarice was awakened at the mention of hidden gold, and she urged her husband to comply with the black man's terms, and secure what would make them wealthy for life. However Tom might have felt disposed to sell himself to the devil, he was determined not to do so to oblige his wife; so he flatly refused, out of the mere spirit of contradiction. Many and bitter were the quarrels they had on the subject; but the more she talked, the more resolute was Tom not to be damned to please her.

At length she determined to drive the bargain on her own

account, and if she succeeded, to keep all the gain to herself. Being of the same fearless temper as her husband, she set off for the old Indian fort towards the close of a summer's day. She was many hours absent. When she came back, she was reserved and sullen in her replies. She spoke something of a black man, whom she met about twilight hewing at the root of a tall tree. He was sulky, however, and would not come to terms: she was to go again with a propitiatory offering, but what it was she forbore to say.

The next evening she set off again for the swamp, with her apron heavily laden. Tom waited and waited for her, but in vain; midnight came, but she did not make her appearance; morning, noon, night returned, but still she did not come. Tom now grew uneasy for her safety, especially as he found she had carried off in her apron the silver tea-pot and spoons, and every portable article of value. Another night elapsed, another morning came; but no wife. She was never heard of more.

What was her real fate nobody knows, in consequence of so many pretending to know. It is one of those facts which have become confounded by a variety of historians. Some asserted that she lost her way among the tangled mazes of the swamp, and sank into some pit or slough; others, more uncharitable, hinted that she had eloped with the household booty, and made off to some other province; while others surmised that the tempter had decoyed her into a dismal quagmire, on the top of which her hat was found lying. In confirmation of this, it was said a great black man, with an axe on his shoulder, was seen

35

late that very evening coming out of the swamp, carrying a bundle tied in a check apron, with an air of surly triumph.

Tom Walker grew so anxious about the fate of his wife and his property, that he set out at length to seek them both at the Indian fort. During a long summer's afternoon he searched about the gloomy place, but no wife was to be seen. He called her name repeatedly, but she was nowhere to be heard. The bittern alone responded to his voice, as he flew screaming by; or the bullfrog croaked dolefully from a neighboring pool. At length, it is said, just in the brown hour of twilight, when the owls began to hoot, and the bats to flit about, his attention was attracted by the clamor of carrion crows hovering about a cypress-tree. He looked up, and beheld a bundle tied in a check apron, and hanging in the branches of the tree, with a great vulture perched hard by, as if keeping watch upon it. He leaped with joy; for he recognized his wife's apron, and supposed it to contain the household valuables.

" Let us get hold of the property," said he, consolingly to himself, " and we will endeavor to do without the woman."

As he scrambled up the tree, the vulture spread its wide wings, and sailed off screaming, into the deep shadows of the forest. Tom seized the checked apron, but, woful sight! found nothing but a heart and liver tied up in it!

Such, according to this most authentic old story, was all that was to be found of Tom's wife. She had probably attempted to deal with the black man as she had been accustomed to deal with her husband; but though a female scold is generally considered a match for the devil, yet in this instance she appears to have had the worst of it. She must have died game, however; for it is said Tom noticed many prints of cloven feet deeply stamped upon the tree, and found handfuls of hair, that looked as if they had been plucked from the coarse black shock of the woodman. Tom knew his wife's prowess by experience. He shrugged his shoulders, as he looked at the signs of a fierce clapper-clawing. " Egad," said he to himself, " Old Scratch must have had a tough time of it! "

Tom consoled himself for the loss of his property, with the loss of his wife, for he was a man of fortitude. He even felt something like gratitude towards the black woodman, who, he considered, had done him a kindness. He sought, therefore, to cultivate a further acquaintance with him, but for some time without success; the old black-legs played shy, for whatever people may think, he is not always to be had for calling for: he knows how to play his cards when pretty sure of his game.

At length, it is said, when delay had whetted Tom's eagerness to the quick, and prepared him to agree to anything rather than not gain the promised treasure, he met the black man one evening in his usual woodman's dress, with his axe on his shoulder, sauntering along the swamp, and humming a tune. He affected to receive Tom's advances with great indifference, made brief replies, and went on humming his tune.

By degrees, however, Tom brought him to business, and they began to haggle about the terms on which the former was to have the pirate's treasure. The devil insisted that the money found through his means should be employed in his service. He proposed, therefore, that Tom should employ it in the black traffic; that is to say, that he should fit out a slave-ship. This, however, Tom resolutely refused: he was bad enough in all conscience; but the devil himself could not tempt him to turn slave-trader.

38

Finding Tom so squeamish on this point, he did not insist upon it, but proposed, instead, that he should turn usurer; the devil being extremely anxious for the increase of usurers, looking upon them as his peculiar people.

To this no objections were made, for it was just to Tom's taste.

"You shall open a broker's shop in Boston next month," said the black man.

" I'll do it to-morrow, if you wish," said Tom Walker.

" You shall lend money at two per cent. a month."

" Egad, I'll charge four! " replied Tom Walker.

" You shall extort bonds, foreclose mortgages, drive the merchants to bankruptcy " —

" I'll drive them to the d——l," cried Tom Walker.

" You are the usurer for my money! " said black-legs with delight. " When will you want the rhino? "

" This very night."

" Done! " said the devil.

" Done! " said Tom Walker. — So they shook hands and struck a bargain.

A few days' time saw Tom Walker seated behind his desk in a counting-house in Boston.

His reputation for a ready-moneyed man, who would lend money out for a good consideration, soon spread abroad. Everybody remembers the time of Governor Belcher, when money was particularly scarce. It was a time of paper credit. The country had been deluged with government bills, the famous Land Bank had been established; there had been a rage for speculating; the people had run mad with schemes for new settlements; for building cities in the wilderness; land-jobbers went about with maps of grants, and townships, and Eldorados, lying nobody knew where, but which everybody was ready to purchase. In a word, the great speculating fever which breaks out every now and then in the country, had raged to an alarming degree, and everybody was dreaming of making sudden fortunes from nothing. As usual the fever had subsided; the

THE AGREEMENT

dream had gone off, and the imaginary fortunes with it; the patients were left in doleful plight, and the whole country resounded with the consequent cry of " hard times."

At this propitious time of public distress did Tom Walker set up as usurer in Boston. His door was soon thronged by customers. The needy and adventurous; the gambling speculator; the dreaming land-jobber; the thriftless tradesman; the merchant with cracked credit; in short, every one driven to raise money by desperate means and desperate sacrifices, hurried to Tom Walker.

Thus Tom was the universal friend of the needy, and acted like a " friend in need "; that is to say, he always exacted good pay and good security. In proportion to the distress of the applicant was the hardness of his terms. He accumulated bonds and mortgages; gradually squeezed his customers closer and closer: and sent them at length, dry as a sponge, from his door.

In this way he made money hand over hand; became a rich and mighty man, and exalted his cocked hat upon 'Change. He built himself, as usual, a vast house, out of ostentation; but left the greater part of it unfinished and unfurnished, out of parsimony. He even set up a carriage in the fulness of his vain-glory, though he nearly starved the horses which drew it; and as the ungreased wheels groaned and screeched on the axle-trees, you would have thought you heard the souls of the poor debtors he was squeezing.

As Tom waxed old, however, he grew thoughtful. Having secured the good things of this world, he began to feel anxious about those of the next. He thought with regret on the bargain he had made with his black friend, and set his wits to work to cheat him out of the conditions. He became, therefore, all of a sudden, a violent church-goer. He prayed loudly and strenuously, as if heaven were to be taken by force of lungs. Indeed, one might always tell when he had sinned most during the week, by the clamor of his Sunday devotion. The quiet Christians who had been modestly and steadfastly travelling Zionward, were struck with self-reproach at seeing themselves so suddenly

43

outstripped in their career by this new-made convert. Tom was as rigid in religious as in money matters; he was a stern supervisor and censurer of his neighbors, and seemed to think every sin entered up to their account became a credit on his own side of the page. He even talked of the expediency of reviving the persecution of Quakers and Anabaptists. In a word, Tom's zeal became as notorious as his riches.

Still, in spite of all this strenuous attention to forms, Tom had a lurking dread that the devil, after all, would have his due. That he might not be taken unawares, therefore, it is said he always carried a small Bible in his coat-pocket. He had also a great folio Bible on his counting-house desk, and would frequently be found reading it when people called on business; on such occasions he would lay his green spectacles in the book, to mark the place, while he turned round to drive some usurious bargain.

Some say that Tom grew a little crack-brained in his old days, and that, fancying his end approaching, he had his horse new shod, saddled and bridled, and buried with his feet uppermost; because he supposed that at the last day the world would be turned upside-down; in which case he should find his horse standing ready for mounting, and he was determined at the worst to give his old friend a run for it. If he really did take such a precaution, it was totally superfluous.

One hot summer afternoon in the dog-days, just as a terrible black thunder gust was coming up, Tom sat in his counting-house, in his white cap and India silk morning-gown. He was on the point of foreclosing a mortgage, by which he would com-

44

plete the ruin of an unlucky land-speculator for whom he had professed the greatest friendship. The poor land-jobber begged him to grant a few months' indulgence. Tom had grown testy and irritated, and refused another day.

" My family will be ruined and brought upon the parish," said the land-jobber. " Charity begins at home," replied Tom; " I must take care of myself in these hard times."

" You have made so much money out of me," said the speculator.

Tom lost his patience and his piety. " The devil take me," said he, " if I have made a farthing! "

Just then there were three loud knocks at the street door. He stepped out to see who was there. A black man was holding a black horse, which neighed and stamped with impatience.

"Tom, you're come for," said the black fellow, gruffly. Tom shrank back, but too late. He had left his little Bible at the bottom of his coat-pocket, and his big Bible on the desk buried under the mortgage he was about to foreclose; never was sinner taken more unawares. The black man whisked him like a child into the saddle, gave the horse the lash, and away he galloped, with Tom on his back, in the midst of the thunder-storm. The

TOM WALKERS RIDE

clerks stuck their pens behind their ears, and stared after him from the windows. Away went Tom Walker, dashing down the streets; his white cap bobbing up and down; his morning-gown fluttering in the wind, and his steed striking fire out of the pavement at every bound. When the clerks turned to look for the black man, he had disappeared.

Tom Walker never returned to foreclose the mortgage. A countryman, who lived on the border of the swamp, reported that in the height of the thunder-gust he had heard a great clattering of hoofs and a howling along the road, and running to the window caught sight of a figure, on a horse that galloped like mad across the fields, over the hills, and down into the black hemlock swamp towards the old Indian fort; shortly after a thunder-bolt falling in that direction seemed to set the whole forest in a blaze.

The good people of Boston shook their heads and shrugged their shoulders, but had been so much accustomed to witches and goblins, and tricks of the devil, in all kinds of shapes, from the first settlement of the colony, that they were not so much horror-struck as might have been expected. Trustees were appointed to take charge of Tom's effects. There was nothing, however, to administer upon. On searching his coffers, all his bonds and mortgages were found reduced to cinders. In place of gold and silver, his iron chest was filled with chips and shavings; two skeletons lay in his stable instead of his half-starved horses, and the very next day his great house took fire and burnt to the ground.

Such was the end of Tom Walker and his ill-gotten wealth.

Let all griping money-brokers lay this story to heart. The truth of it is not to be doubted. The very hole under the oak-trees whence he dug Kidd's money is to be seen to this day; and the neighboring swamp and old Indian fort are often haunted in stormy nights by a figure on horseback, in morning-gown and white cap, which is doubtless the troubled spirit of the usurer. In fact the story has resolved itself into a proverb, and is the origin of that popular saying, so prevalent throughout New England, of " The Devil and Tom Walker."

WOLFERT WEBBER

Wolfert Webber or Golden Dreams

IN THE year of grace one thousand seven hundred and — blank — there lived in the ancient city of the Manhattoes a worthy burgher, Wolfert Webber by name. He was descended from old Cobus Webber of the Brille in Holland, one of the original settlers, famous for introducing the cultivation of cabbages, and who came over to the province during the protectorship of Oloffe Van Kortlandt, otherwise called the Dreamer.

The field in which Cobus Webber first planted himself and his cabbages had remained ever since in the family. The whole family genius, during several generations, was devoted to the study and development of this one noble vegetable; and to this concentration of intellect may doubtless be ascribed the prodigious renown to which the Webber cabbages attained.

The Webber dynasty continued in uninterrupted succession; and never did a line give more unquestionable proofs of legitimacy. The eldest son succeeded to the looks, as well as the territory of his sire; and had the portraits of this line of tranquil potentates been taken, they would have presented a row of heads marvellously resembling in shape and magnitude the vegetables over which they reigned.

The seat of government continued unchanged in the family mansion — a Dutch-built house, with a front, or rather gable-end of yellow brick, tapering to a point, with the customary iron weathercock at the top. Everything about the building bore the air of long-settled ease and security. Flights of martins peopled the little coops nailed against its walls, and swallows built their nests under the eaves; and every one knows that these house-loving birds bring good luck to the dwelling where they take up their abode. In a bright morning in early summer, it was delectable to hear their cheerful notes, as they sported about in the pure sweet air, chirping forth, as it were, the greatness and prosperity of the Webbers.

Thus quietly and comfortably did this excellent family vegetate under the shade of a mighty button-wood tree, which, by little and little, grew so great as entirely to overshadow their palace. The city gradually spread its suburbs round their domain. Houses sprang up to interrupt their prospects. The rural lanes in the vicinity began to grow into the bustle and populousness of streets; in short, with all the habits of rustic life they began to find themselves the inhabitants of a city. Wolfert was the last of the line, and succeeded to the patriarchal bench at the door, under the family tree, and swayed the sceptre of his fathers, a kind of rural potentate in the midst of the metropolis.

To share the cares and sweets of sovereignty, he had taken unto himself a helpmate, one of that excellent kind called stirring women; that is to say, she was one of those notable little house-wives who are always busy where there is nothing to do. Her activity, however, took one particular direction: her whole life seemed devoted to intense knitting; whether at home or abroad, walking or sitting, her needles were continually in motion, and it is even affirmed that by her unwearied industry she very nearly supplied her household with stockings throughout the year. This worthy couple were blessed with one daughter, who was brought up with great tenderness and care; uncommon pains had been taken with her education, so that she could stitch every variety of way; make all kinds of pickles and preserves, and mark her own name on a sampler. The influence of her taste was seen also in the family garden, where the ornamental began to mingle with the useful; whole rows of fiery marigolds and splendid hollyhocks bordered the cabbage-beds; and gigantic sunflowers lolled their broad jolly faces over the fences, seeming to ogle most affectionately the passers-by.

Thus reigned and vegetated Wolfert Webber over his paternal acres, peacefully and contentedly. Not but that, like all other sovereigns, he had his occasional cares and vexations. The growth of his native city sometimes caused him annoyance. His little territory gradually became hemmed in by streets and houses, which intercepted air and sunshine. He was now and then subjected to the irruptions of the border population that infest the streets of a metropolis; who would make midnight forays into his dominions, and carry off captive whole platoons of his noblest subjects. Vagrant swine would make a descent, too, now and then, when the gate was left open, and lay all waste before them; and mischievous urchins would decapitate the illustrious sunflowers, the glory of the garden, as they lolled their heads so fondly over the walls. Still all these were petty grievances, which might now and then ruffle the surface of his mind, as a summer breeze will ruffle the surface of a mill-pond;

but they could not disturb the deep-seated quiet of his soul. He would but seize a trusty staff, that stood behind the door, issue suddenly out, and anoint the back of the aggressor, whether pig or urchin, and then return within doors, marvellously refreshed and tranquillized.

The chief cause of anxiety to honest Wolfert, however, was the growing prosperity of the city. The expense of living doubled and trebled; but he could not double and treble the magnitude of his cabbages; and the number of competitors prevented the increase of price; thus, while every one around him grew richer, Wolfert grew poorer, and he could not, for the life of him, perceive how the evil was to be remedied.

This growing care, which increased from day to day, had its gradual effect upon our worthy burgher; insomuch, that it at length implanted two or three wrinkles in his brow; things unknown before in the family of the Webbers; and it seemed to pinch up the corners of his cocked hat into an expression of anxiety, totally opposite to the tranquil, broad-brimmed, low-crowned beavers of his illustrious progenitors.

Perhaps even this would not have materially disturbed the serenity of his mind, had he had only himself and his wife to care for; but there was his daughter gradually growing to maturity; and all the world knows that when daughters begin to ripen, no fruit nor flower requires so much looking after. I have no talent at describing female charms, else fain would I depict the progress of this little Dutch beauty. How her blue eyes grew deeper and deeper, and her cherry lips redder and redder; and how she ripened and ripened, and rounded and rounded in the opening breath of sixteen summers, until, in her seventeenth spring, she seemed ready to burst out of her bodice, like a half-blown rose-bud.

Ah, well-a-day! could I but show her as she was then, tricked out on a Sunday morning, in the hereditary finery of the old Dutch clothes-press, of which her mother had confided to her the key. The wedding-dress of her grandmother, modern-ized for use, with sundry ornaments, handed down as heirlooms in the family. Her pale brown hair smoothed with buttermilk in flat waving lines on each side of her fair forehead. The chain of yellow virgin gold, that encircled her neck; the little cross, that just rested at the entrance of a soft valley of happiness, as if it would sanctify the place.

At this critical period of female existence, when the heart within a damsel's bosom, like its emblem, the miniature which hangs without, is apt to be engrossed by a single image, a new visitor began to make his appearance under the roof of Wolfert Webber. This was Dirk Waldron, the only son of a poor widow, but who could boast of more fathers than any lad in the prov-ince; for his mother had had four husbands, and this only child; so that though born in her last wedlock, he might fairly claim to be the tardy fruit of a long course of cultivation. This son of four fathers united the merits and the vigors of all his sires. If he had not had a great family before him, he seemed likely to have a great one after him; for you had only to look at the fresh bucksome youth, to see that he was formed to be the founder of a mighty race.

This youngster gradually became an intimate visitor of the

family. He talked little, but he sat long. He filled the father's pipe when it was empty, gathered up the mother's knitting-needle, or ball of worsted when it fell to the ground; stroked the sleek coat of the tortoise-shell cat, and replenished the tea-pot for the daughter from the bright copper kettle that sang before the fire. All these quiet little offices may seem of trifling import; but when true love is translated into Low Dutch, it is in this way that it eloquently expresses itself. They were not lost upon the Webber family. The winning youngster found marvellous favor in the eyes of the mother; the tortoise-shell cat, albeit the most staid and demure of her kind, gave indubitable signs of approbation of his visits; the tea-kettles seemed to sing out a cheering note of welcome at his approach; and if the sly glances of the daughter might be rightly read, as she sat bridling and dimpling, and sewing by her mother's side, she was not a whit behind Dame Webber, or grimalkin, or the tea-kettle, in good-will.

Wolfert alone saw nothing of what was going on. Profoundly wrapt up in meditation on the growth of the city and his cabbages, he sat looking in the fire, and puffing his pipe in silence. One night, however, as the gentle Amy, according to custom, lighted her lover to the outer door, and he, according to custom, took his parting salute, the smack resounded so vigorously through the long silent entry, as to startle even the dull ear of Wolfert. He was slowly roused to a new source of anxiety. It had never entered into his head that this mere child, who, as it seemed, but the other day had been climbing about his knees, and playing with dolls and baby-houses, could all at

58

once be thinking of lovers and matrimony. He rubbed his eyes, examined into the fact, and really found that, while he had been dreaming of other matters, she had actually grown to be a woman, and, what was worse, had fallen in love. Here arose new cares for Wolfert. He was a kind father, but he was a prudent man. The young man was a lively, stirring lad; but then he had neither money nor land. Wolfert's ideas all ran in one channel; and he saw no alternative in case of a marriage but to portion off the young couple with a corner of his cabbage-garden, the whole of which was barely sufficient for the support of his family.

Like a prudent father, therefore, he determined to nip this passion in the bud, and forbade the youngster the house; though sorely did it go against his fatherly heart, and many a silent tear did it cause in the bright eye of his daughter. She showed herself, however, a pattern of filial piety and obedience. She never pouted and sulked; never flew in the face of parental authority; she never flew into a passion, nor fell into hysterics, as many romantic novel-read young ladies would do. On the contrary, she acquiesced like an obedient daughter, shut the street-door in her lover's face, and if ever she did grant him an interview, it was either out of the kitchen-window, or over the garden-fence.

Wolfert was deeply cogitating these matters in his mind, and his brow wrinkled with unusual care, as he wended his way one Saturday afternoon to a rural inn, about two miles from the city. It was a favorite resort of the Dutch part of the community, from being always held by a Dutch line of landlords, and retaining an air and relish of the good old times. It was a

Dutch-built house, that had probably been a country seat of some opulent burgher in the early time of the settlement. It stood near a point of land called Corlaer's Hook, which stretches out into the Sound, and against which the tide, at its flux and reflux, sets with extraordinary rapidity. The venerable and somewhat crazy mansion was distinguished from afar by a grove of elms and sycamores that seemed to wave a hospitable invitation, while a few weeping-willows, with their dank, drooping foliage, resembling falling waters, gave an idea of coolness, that rendered it an attractive spot during the heat of the summer.

Here resorted many of the old inhabitants of the Manhattoes, while some played at shuffle-board and quoits and nine-pins, others smoked a deliberate pipe and talked over public affairs.

It was on a blustering autumnal afternoon that Wolfert made his visit to the inn. The nine-pin alley was deserted, for the premature chilliness of the day had driven the company within doors. As it was Saturday afternoon, the habitual club was in session, composed principally of regular Dutch burghers, though mingled occasionally with persons of various character and country, as is natural in a place of such motley population.

Beside the fireplace, in a huge leather-bottomed arm-chair, sat the dictator of this little world, the venerable Rem, or, as it was pronounced, Ramm Rapelye. He was a man of Walloon race, and illustrious for the antiquity of his line; his great-grandmother having been the first white child born in the province. But he was still more illustrious for his wealth and dignity: he had long filled the noble office of alderman, and was a man to whom the governor himself took off his hat. He had maintained possession of the leather-bottomed chair from time immemorial; and had gradually waxed in bulk as he sat in his seat of government, until in the course of years he filled its whole magnitude. His word was decisive with his subjects; for he was so rich a man that he was never expected to support any opinion by argument. The landlord had ever a pleasant word and a joke to insinuate in the ear of the august Ramm. It is true, Ramm never laughed, and, indeed, ever maintained a mastiff-like gravity, and even surliness of aspect; yet he now and then rewarded mine host with a token of approbation; which, though nothing more nor less than a kind of a grunt, still delighted the landlord more than a broad laugh from a poorer man.

" This will be a rough night for the money-diggers," said mine host, as a gust of wind howled round the house, and rattled at the windows.

61

"What, are they at their works again?" said an English half-pay captain, with one eye, who was a very frequent attendant at the inn.

"Aye, are they," said the landlord, "and well may they be. They've had luck of late. They say a great pot of money has been dug up in the fields, just behind Stuyvesant's orchard. Folks think it must have been buried there in old times, by Peter Stuyvesant, the Dutch governor."

"Fudge!" said the one-eyed man of war, as he added a small portion of water to a bottom of brandy.

"Well, you may believe it or not, as you please," said mine host, somewhat nettled; "but everybody knows that the old governor buried a great deal of his money at the time of the Dutch troubles, when the English red-coats seized on the province. They say, too, the old gentleman walks; aye, and in the very same dress that he wears in the picture that hangs up in the family house."

"Fudge!" said the half-pay officer.

"Fudge, if you please! — But didn't Corney Van Zandt see him at midnight, stalking about in the meadow with his wooden leg, and a drawn sword in his hand, that flashed like fire? And what can he be walking for, but because people have been troubling the place where he buried his money in old times?"

Here the landlord was interrupted by several guttural sounds from Ramm Rapelye, betokening that he was laboring with the unusual production of an idea. As he was too great a man to be slighted by a prudent publican, mine host respect-

62

fully paused until he should deliver himself; every portion of his speech being marked by a testy puff of tobacco smoke.

"Who talks of old Peter Stuyvesant's walking? — puff — Have people no respect for persons? — puff — puff — Peter Stuyvesant knew better what to do with his money than to bury it — puff — I know the Stuyvesant family — puff — every one of them — puff — not a more respectable family in the province — puff — old standards — puff — warm householders — puff — none of your upstarts — puff — puff — puff —. Don't talk to me of Peter Stuyvesant's walking — puff — puff — puff — puff."

Here the redoubtable Ramm contracted his brow, clasped up his mouth, till it wrinkled at each corner, and redoubled his smoking with such vehemence, that the cloudy volumes soon wreathed round his head, as the smoke envelopes the awful summit of Mount Ætna.

A general silence followed the sudden rebuke of this very rich man. The subject, however, was too interesting to be readily abandoned. The conversation soon broke forth again from the lips of Peechy Prauw Van Hook, the chronicler of the club, one of those prosing, narrative old men who seem to be troubled with an incontinence of words, as they grow old.

Peechy could, at any time, tell as many stories in an evening as his hearers could digest in a month. He now resumed the conversation, by affirming that, to his knowledge, money had, at different times, been digged up in various parts of the island. The lucky persons who had discovered them had always dreamt of them three times beforehand, and what was worthy of remark, those treasures had never been found but by some descendant of the good old Dutch families, which clearly proved that they had been buried by Dutchmen in the olden time.

" Fiddlestick with your Dutchmen! " cried the half-pay officer. " The Dutch had nothing to do with them. They were all buried by Kidd the pirate, and his crew."

Here a key-note was touched that roused the whole company. The name of Captain Kidd was like a talisman in those times, and was associated with a thousand marvellous stories.

The half-pay officer took the lead, and in his narrations fathered upon Kidd all the plunderings and exploits of Morgan, Blackbeard, and the whole list of bloody buccaneers.

The officer was a man of great weight among the peaceable members of the club, by reason of his warlike character and gunpowder tales. All his golden stories of Kidd, however, and of the booty he had buried, were obstinately rivalled by the tales of Peechy Prauw, who, rather than suffer his Dutch progenitors to be eclipsed by a foreign freebooter, enriched every field and shore in the neighborhood with the hidden wealth of Peter Stuyvesant and his contemporaries.

Not a word of this conversation was lost upon Wolfert Webber. He returned pensively home, full of magnificent ideas.

The soil of his native island seemed to be turned into gold dust; and every field to teem with treasure. His head almost reeled at the thought how often he must have heedlessly rambled over places where countless sums lay, scarcely covered by the turf beneath his feet. His mind was in an uproar with this whirl of new ideas. As he came in sight of the venerable mansion of his forefathers, and the little realm where the Webbers had so long, and so contentedly flourished, his gorge rose at the narrowness of his destiny.

" Unlucky Wolfert! " exclaimed he; " others can go to bed and dream themselves into whole mines of wealth; they have but to seize a spade in the morning, and turn up doubloons like potatoes; but thou must dream of hardships, and rise to poverty, — must dig thy field from year's end to year's end, and yet raise nothing but cabbages! "

Wolfert Webber went to bed with a heavy heart; and it was long before the golden visions that disturbed his brain permitted him to sink into repose. The same visions, however, extended into his sleeping thoughts, and assumed a more definite form. He dreamt that he had discovered an immense treasure in the centre of his garden. At every stroke of the spade he laid bare a golden ingot; diamond crosses sparkled out of the dust; bags of money turned up their bellies, corpulent with pieces-of-eight, or venerable doubloons; and chests, wedged close with moidores, ducats, and pistareens, yawned before his ravished eyes, and vomited forth their glittering contents.

Wolfert awoke a poorer man than ever. He had no heart to go about his daily concerns, which appeared so paltry and

65

profitless; but sat all day long in the chimney-corner, picturing to himself ingots and heaps of gold in the fire. The next night his dream was repeated. He was again in his garden, digging, and laying open stores of hidden wealth. There was something very singular in this repetition. He passed another day of reverie, and though it was cleaning-day, and the house, as usual in Dutch households, completely topsy-turvy, yet he sat unmoved amidst the general uproar.

The third night he went to bed with a palpitating heart. He put on his red night-cap wrong-side outwards, for good luck. It was deep mid-night before his anxious mind could settle itself into sleep. Again the golden dream was repeated, and again he saw his garden teeming with ingots and money-bags.

Wolfert rose the next morning in complete bewilderment. A dream, three times repeated, was never known to lie; and if so, his fortune was made.

In his agitation he put on his waistcoat with the hind part before, and this was a corroboration of good luck. He no longer doubted that a huge store of money lay buried somewhere in his cabbage-field, coyly waiting to be sought for; and he repined at having so long been scratching about the surface of the soil instead of digging to the centre.

He took his seat at the breakfast-table full of these speculations; asked his daughter to put a lump of gold into his tea, and on handing his wife a plate of slap-jacks, begged her to help herself to a doubloon.

His grand care now was how to secure this immense treasure without its being known. Instead of his working regularly in his grounds in the daytime, he now stole from his bed at night, and with spade and pickaxe went to work to rip up and dig about his paternal acres, from one end to the other. In a little time the whole garden, which had presented such a goodly and regular appearance, with its phalanx of cabbages, like a vegetable army in battle array, was reduced to a scene of devastation; while the relentless Wolfert, with night-cap on head, and lantern and spade in hand, stalked through the slaughtered ranks, the destroying angel of his own vegetable world.

Every morning bore testimony to the ravages of the preceding night in cabbages of all ages and conditions, from the tender sprout to the full-grown head, piteously rooted from their quiet beds like worthless weeds, and left to wither in the sunshine. In vain Wolfert's wife remonstrated; in vain his darling daughter wept over the destruction of some favorite marigold. " Thou shalt have gold of another guess sort," he would say, chucking her under the chin; " thou shalt have a string of crooked ducats for thy wedding necklace, my child." His family began really to fear that the poor man's wits were diseased. He muttered in his sleep at night about mines of wealth, about pearls and diamonds, and bars of gold. In the daytime he was moody and abstracted, and walked about as if in a trance. Dame Webber held frequent councils with all the old women of the neighborhood; scarce an hour in the day but a knot of them might be seen wagging their white caps together round her door, while the poor woman made some piteous recital. The daughter, too, was fain to seek for more frequent consolation from the stolen interviews of her favored swain, Dirk Waldron. The delectable little Dutch songs with which she used to dulcify the house grew less and less frequent, and she would forget her sewing, and look wistfully in her father's face as he sat pondering by the fireside. Wolfert caught her eye one day fixed on him thus anxiously, and for a moment was roused from his golden reveries. — " Cheer up, my girl," said he, exultingly; " why dost thou droop? — thou shalt hold up thy head one day with the Brinckerhoffs, and the Schermerhorns, the Van Hornes, and the Van Dams. By Saint Nicholas, but the patroon himself shall be glad to get thee for his son! "

Amy shook her head at his vainglorious boast, and was more than ever in doubt of the soundness of the good man's intellect.

In the meantime Wolfert went on digging and digging; but the field was extensive, and as his dream had indicated no precise spot, he had to dig at random. The winter set in before one tenth of the scene of promise had been explored.

The ground became frozen hard, and the nights too cold for the labors of the spade.

No sooner did the returning warmth of spring loosen the soil, and the small frogs begin to pipe in the meadows, but Wolfert resumed his labors with renovated zeal. Still, however, the hours of industry were reversed.

Instead of working cheerily all day, planting and setting out his vegetables, he remained thoughtfully idle, until the shades of night summoned him to his secret labors. In this way he continued to dig from night to night, and week to

week, and month to month, but not a stiver did he find. On the contrary, the more he digged, the poorer he grew. The rich soil of his garden was digged away, and the sand and gravel from beneath was thrown to the surface, until the whole field presented an aspect of sandy barrenness.

In the meantime, the seasons gradually rolled on. The little frogs which had piped in the meadows in early spring, croaked as bull-frogs during the summer heats, and then sank into silence. The peach-tree budded, blossomed, and bore its fruit. The swallows and martins came, twitted about the roof, built their nests, reared their young, held their congress along the eaves, and then winged their flight in search of another spring. The caterpillar spun its winding-sheet, dangled it from the great button-wood tree before the house; turned into a moth, fluttered with the last sunshine of summer, and disappeared; and finally the leaves of the button-wood tree turned yellow, then brown, then rustled one by one to the ground, and whirling about in little eddies of wind and dust, whispered that winter was at hand.

Wolfert gradually woke from his dream of wealth as the year declined. He had reared no crop for the supply of his household during the sterility of winter. The season was long and severe, and for the first time the family was really straitened in its comforts. By degrees a revulsion of thought took place in Wolfert's mind, common to those whose golden dreams have been disturbed by pinching realities. The idea gradually stole upon him that he should come to want. He already considered himself one of the most unfortunate men in the province, having lost such an incalculable amount of undiscovered treasure, and now, when thousands of pounds had eluded his search, to be perplexed for shillings and pence, was cruel in the extreme.

Haggard care gathered about his brow; he went about with a money-seeking air, his eyes bent downwards into the dust, and carrying his hands in his pockets, as men are apt to do when they have nothing else to put into them. He could not even pass the city almshouse without giving it a rueful glance, as if destined to be his future abode.

The strangeness of his conduct and of his looks occasioned much speculation and remark. For a long time he was suspected of being crazy, and then everybody pitied him; and at length it began to be suspected that he was poor, and then everybody avoided him.

The rich old burghers of his acquaintance met him outside of the door when he called, entertained him hospitably on the threshold, pressed him warmly by the hand at parting, shook their heads as he walked away, with the kind-hearted expression of "poor Wolfert," and turned a corner nimbly if by chance they saw him approaching as they walked the streets. Even the barber and the cobbler of the neighborhood, and a tattered tailor in an alley hard by, three of the poorest and merriest rogues in the world, eyed him with that abundant sympathy which usually attends a lack of means; and there is not a doubt but their pockets would have been at his command, only that they happened to be empty.

Thus everybody deserted the Webber mansion, as if poverty were contagious, like the plague; everybody but honest Dirk Waldron, who still kept up his stolen visits to the daughter, and indeed seemed to wax more affectionate as the fortunes of his mistress were in the wane.

Many months had elapsed since Wolfert had frequented his old resort, the rural inn. He was taking a long lonely walk one Saturday afternoon, musing over his wants and disappointments, when his feet took instinctively their wonted direction, and on awaking out of a reverie, he found himself before the door of the inn. For some moments he hesitated whether to enter, but his heart yearned for companionship; and where can a ruined man find better companionship than at a tavern, where there is neither sober example nor sober advice to put him out of countenance?

Wolfert found several of the old frequenters of the inn at their usual places; but one was missing, the great Ramm Rapelye, who for many years had filled the leather-bottomed chair of state. His place was supplied by a stranger, who seemed, however, completely at home in the chair and the tavern. He was rather under size, but deep-chested, square, and muscular. His broad shoulders, double joints, and bow knees, gave tokens of prodigious strength. His face was dark and weather-beaten; a deep scar, as if from the slash of a cutlass, had almost divided his nose, and made a gash in his upper lip, through which his teeth shone like a bull-dog's. A mop of iron-gray hair gave a grisly finish to this hard-favored visage. His dress was of an amphibious character. He wore an old hat edged with tarnished lace, and cocked in martial style,

71

on one side of his head; a rusty blue military coat with brass buttons, and a wide pair of short petticoat trousers, or rather breeches, for they were gathered up at the knees. He ordered everybody about him with an authoritative air; talking in a brattling voice, that sounded like the crackling of thorns under a pot; d—d the landlord and servants with perfect impunity, and was waited upon with greater obsequiousness than had ever been shown to the mighty Ramm himself.

Wolfert's curiosity was awakened to know who and what was this stranger, who had thus usurped absolute sway in this ancient domain. Peechy Prauw took him aside, into a remote corner of the hall, and there, in an under voice, and with great caution, imparted to him all that he knew on the subject. The inn had been aroused several months before, on a dark night, by repeated long shouts, that seemed like the howling of a wolf. They came from the water-side and at length were distinguished to be hailing the house in the seafaring manner, " House-a-hoy! " The landlord turned out with his head waiter, tapster, hostler, and errand-boy, — that is to say, with his old negro Cuff. On approaching the place whence the voice proceeded, they found this amphibious-looking personage at the water's edge, quite alone, and seated on a great oaken sea-chest. How he came there, whether he had been set on shore from some boat, or had floated to land on his chest, nobody could tell, for he did not seem disposed to answer questions; and there was something in his looks and manners that put a stop to all questioning. Suffice it to say, he took possession of a

corner-room of the inn, to which his chest was removed with great difficulty. Here he had remained ever since, keeping about the inn and its vicinity. Sometimes, it is true, he disappeared for one, two, or three days at a time, going and returning without giving any notice or account of his movements. He always appeared to have plenty of money, though often of very strange, outlandish coinage; and he regularly paid his bill every evening before turning in.

He had fitted up his room to his own fancy, having slung a hammock from the ceiling instead of a bed, and decorated the walls with rusty pistols and cutlasses of foreign workmanship. A greater part of his time was passed in this room, seated by the window, which commanded a wide view of the Sound, a short old-fashioned pipe in his mouth, a glass of rum-toddy at his elbow, and a pocket-telescope in his hand, with which he reconnoitred every boat that moved upon the water. Large, square-rigged vessels seemed to excite but little attention; but the moment he descried anything with a shoulder-of-mutton sail, or that a barge, or yawl, or jolly-boat hove in sight, up went the telescope, and he examined it with the most scrupulous attention.

All this might have passed without much notice, for in those times the province was so much the resort of adventurers of all characters and climes, that any oddity in dress or behavior attracted but small attention. In a little while, however, this strange sea-monster, thus strangely cast upon dry land, began to encroach upon the long-established customs and customers of the place, and to interfere in a dictatorial manner in the affairs of the nine-pin alley and the bar-room, until in the end he usurped an absolute command over the whole inn. It was all in vain to attempt to withstand his authority. He was not exactly quarrelsome, but boisterous and peremptory, like one accustomed to tyrannize on a quarter-deck; and there was a dare-devil air about everything he said and did, that inspired wariness in all by-standers. Even the half-pay officer, so long the hero of the club, was soon silenced by him; and the quiet burghers stared with wonder at seeing their inflammable man-of-war so readily and quietly extinguished.

And then the tales that he would tell were enough to make a peaceable man's hair stand on end. There was not a sea-fight, nor marauding nor freebooting adventure that had happened within the last twenty years, but he seemed perfectly versed in it. He delighted to talk of the exploits of the buccaneers in the West Indies, and on the Spanish Main. How his eyes would glisten, as he described the waylaying of treasure-ships, the desperate fights, yard-arm and yard-arm — broadside and broadside — the boarding and capturing huge Spanish galleons! With what chuckling relish would he describe the descent upon some rich Spanish colony; the rifling of a church; the sacking of a convent! You would have thought you heard some gormandizer dilating upon the roasting of a savory goose at Michaelmas as he described the roasting of some Spanish Don to make him discover his treasure — a detail given with a minuteness that made every rich old burgher present turn uncomfortably in his chair. All this would be told with infinite glee, as if he considered it an excellent joke; and then he would give such a tyrannical leer in the face of his next neighbor, that the poor man would be fain to laugh out of sheer faintheartedness. If any one, however, pretended to contradict him in any of his stories, he was on fire in an instant. His very cocked hat assumed a momentary fierceness, and seemed to resent the contradiction. " How the devil should you know as well as I? — I tell you it was as I say; " and he would at the same time let slip a broadside of thundering oaths and tremendous sea-phrases, such as had never been heard before within these peaceful walls.

Indeed, the worthy burghers began to surmise that he knew more of those stories than mere hearsay. Day after day their conjectures concerning him grew more and more wild and fearful. The strangeness of his arrival, the strangeness of his manners, the mystery that surrounded him, all made him something incomprehensible in their eyes. He was a kind of monster of the deep to them — he was a merman — he was

a behemoth — he was a leviathan — in short, they knew not what he was.

The domineering spirit of this boisterous sea-urchin at length grew quite intolerable. He was no respecter of persons; he contradicted the richest burghers without hesitation; he took possession of the sacred elbow-chair, which, time out of mind, had been the seat of sovereignty of the illustrious Ramm Rapelye. Nay, he even went so far, in one of his rough jocular moods, as to slap that mighty burgher on the back, drink his toddy, and wink in his face, a thing scarcely to be believed. From this time Ramm Rapelye appeared no more at the inn; his example was followed by several of the most eminent customers, who were too rich to tolerate being bullied out of their opinions, or being obliged to laugh at another man's jokes. The landlord was almost in despair; but he knew not how to get rid of this sea-monster and his sea-chest, who seemed both to have grown like fixtures, or excrescences, on his establishment.

Such was the account whispered cautiously in Wolfert's ear, by the narrator, Peechy Prauw, as he held him by the button in a corner of the hall, casting a wary glance now and then towards the door of the bar-room, lest he should be overheard by the terrible hero of his tale.

Wolfert took his seat in a remote part of the room in silence; impressed with profound awe of this unknown, so versed in freebooting history. It was to him a wonderful instance of the revolutions of mighty empires, to find the venerable Ramm Rapelye thus ousted from the throne, and a rugged tarpauling dictating from his elbow-chair, hectoring the patriarchs, and filling this tranquil little realm with brawl and bravado.

The stranger was on this evening in a more than usually communicative mood, and was narrating a number of astounding stories of plunderings and burnings on the high seas. He dwelt upon them with peculiar relish, heightening the frightful particulars in proportion to their effect on his peaceful auditors. He gave a swaggering detail of the capture of a Spanish merchantman. She was lying becalmed during a long summer's day, just off from the island which was one of the lurking-places of the pirates. They had reconnoitered her with their spy-glasses from the shore, and ascertained her character and force. At night a picked crew of daring fellows set off for her in a whale-boat. They approached with muffled oars, as she lay rocking idly with the undulations of the sea, and her sails flapping against the masts. They were close under the stern before the guard on deck was aware of their approach. The alarm was given; the pirates threw hand-grenades on deck, and sprang up the main chains, sword in hand.

The crew flew to arms, but in great confusion; some were shot down, others took refuge in the tops; others were driven overboard and drowned, while others fought hand to hand from the main-deck to the quarter-deck, disputing gallantly every inch of ground. There were three Spanish gentlemen on board with their ladies, who made the most desperate resistance. They defended the companion-way, cut down several of their assailants, and fought like very devils, for they were maddened by the shrieks of the ladies from the cabin. One of the Dons was old, and soon dispatched. The other two kept their ground vigorously, even though the captain of the pirates was among their assailants. Just then there was a shout of victory from the main-deck. " The ship is ours! " cried the pirates. One of the Dons immediately dropped his sword and surrendered; the other, who was a hot-headed youngster, and just married, gave the captain a slash in the face that laid it all open. The captain just made out to articulate the words " no quarter."

" And what did they do with their prisoners? " said Peechy Prauw, eagerly.

" Threw them all overboard," was the answer. A dead pause followed the reply. Peechy Prauw sunk quietly back, like a man who had unwarily stolen upon the lair of a sleeping lion. The honest burghers cast fearful glances at the deep scar slashed across the visage of the stranger, and moved their chairs a little farther off. The seaman, however, smoked on without moving a muscle, as though he either did not perceive or did not regard the unfavorable effect he had produced upon his hearers.

The half-pay officer was the first to break the silence; for he was continually tempted to make ineffectual head against this tyrant of the seas, and to regain his lost consequence in the eyes of his ancient companions. He now tried to match the gunpowder tales of the stranger by others equally tremendous. Kidd, as usual, was his hero, concerning whom he seemed to have picked up many of the floating traditions of the province. The seaman had always evinced a settled pique against the one-eyed warrior. On this occasion he listened with peculiar impatience. He sat with arm akimbo, the other elbow on the table, the hand holding on to the small pipe he was pettishly puffing; his legs crossed; drumming with one foot on the ground, and casting every now and then the side-glance of a basilisk at the prosing captain. At length the latter spoke of Kidd's having ascended the Hudson with some of his crew, to land his plunder in secrecy.

"Kidd up the Hudson!" burst forth the seaman, with a tremendous oath, — "Kidd never was up the Hudson!"

"I tell you he was," said the other. "Aye, and they say he buried a quantity of treasure on the little flat that runs out into the river, called the Devil's Dans Kammer."

"The Devil's Dans Kammer in your teeth!" cried the seaman. "I tell you Kidd never was up the Hudson. What a plague do you know of Kidd and his haunts?"

"What do I know?" echoed the half-pay officer. "Why, I was in London at the time of his trial; aye, and I had the pleasure of seeing him hanged at Execution Dock."

"Then, sir, let me tell you that you saw as pretty a fellow hanged as ever trod shoe-leather. Aye!" putting his face nearer to that of the officer, "and there was many a land-lubber looked on that might much better have swung in his stead."

The half-pay officer was silenced; but the indignation thus pent up in his bosom glowed with intense vehemence in his single eye, which kindled like a coal.

Peechy Prauw, who never could remain silent, observed

that the gentleman certainly was in the right. Kidd never did bury money up the Hudson, nor indeed in any of those parts, though many affirmed such to be the fact. It was Bradish and others of the buccaneers who had buried money; some said in Turtle Bay, others in Long Island, others in the neighborhood of Hell Gate. " Indeed," added he, " I recollect an adventure of Sam, the negro fisherman, many years ago, which some think had something to do with the buccaneers. As we are all friends here, and as it will go no further, I'll tell it to you.

" Upon a dark night many years ago, as Black Sam was returning from fishing in Hell Gate — "

Here the story was nipped in the bud by a sudden movement from the unknown, who laying his iron fist on the table, knuckles downward, with a quiet force that indented the very boards, and looking grimly over his shoulder, with the grin of an angry bear, — " Heark'ee neighbor," said he, with a significant nodding of the head, " you'd better let the buccaneers and their money alone, — they're not for old men and old women to meddle with. They fought hard for their money; they gave body and soul for it; and wherever it lies buried, depend upon it he must have a tug with the devil who gets it! "

This sudden explosion was succeeded by a blank silence throughout the room. Peechy Prauw shrunk within himself, and even the one-eyed officer turned pale. Wolfert, who from a dark corner of the room had listened with intense eagerness to all this talk about buried treasure, looked with mingled awe and reverence at this bold buccaneer; for such he really suspected him to be. There was a chinking of gold and a

81

sparkling of jewels in all his stories about the Spanish Main that gave a value to every period; and Wolfert would have given anything for the rummaging of the ponderous sea-chest, which his imagination crammed full of golden chalices, crucifixes, and jolly round bags of doubloons.

The dead stillness that had fallen upon the company was at length interrupted by the stranger, who pulled out a prodigious watch of curious and ancient workmanship, and which in Wolfert's eyes had a decidedly Spanish look. On touching a spring it struck ten o'clock; upon which the sailor called for his reckoning, and having paid it out of a handful of outlandish coin, he drank off the remainder of his beverage, and without taking leave of any one, rolled out of the room, muttering to himself, as he stamped upstairs to his chamber.

It was some time before the company could recover from the silence into which they had been thrown. The very footsteps of the stranger, which were heard now and then as he traversed his chamber, inspired awe.

A heavy thunder-gust had gathered up unnoticed while they were lost in talk, and the torrents of rain that fell forbade all thoughts of setting off for home until the storm should subside. They drew nearer together, therefore, and entreated the worthy Peechy Prauw to continue the tale which had been so discourteously interrupted. He readily complied, whispering, however, in a tone scarcely above his breath, and drowned occasionally by the rolling of the thunder; and he would pause every now and then, and listen with evident awe, as he heard the heavy footsteps of the stranger pacing overhead.

82

The Adventure of the Black Fisherman

The Adventure of the Black Fisherman

EVERYBODY KNOWS Black Sam, the old negro fisherman, or, as he is commonly called, Mud Sam, who has fished about the Sound for the last half century. It is now many years since Sam, who was then as active a young negro as any in the province, and worked on the farm of Killian Suydam on Long Island, having finished his day's work at an early hour, was fishing, one still summer evening, just about the neighborhood of Hell Gate.

He was in a light skiff; and being well acquainted with the currents and eddies, had shifted his station according to the shifting of the tide, from the Hen and Chickens to the Hog's Back, from the Hog's Back to the Pot, and from the Pot to the Frying-Pan; but in the eagerness of his sport he did not see that the tide was rapidly ebbing, until the roaring of the whirlpools and eddies warned him of his danger; and he had some difficulty in shooting his skiff from among the rocks and breakers, and getting to the point of Blackwell's Island. Here he cast anchor for some time, waiting the turn of the tide to enable him to return homewards. As the night set in, it grew blustering and gusty. Dark clouds came bundling up in the west; and now and then a growl of thunder or a flash of lightning told that a summer storm was at hand. Sam pulled over, therefore, under the lee of Manhattan Island, and coasting along, came to a snug nook, just under a steep beetling rock, where he fastened his skiff to the root of a tree that shot out from a cleft, and spread its broad branches like a canopy over the water. The gust came scouring along; the wind threw up the river in white surges; the rain rattled among the leaves; the thunder bellowed worse than that which is now bellowing; the lightning seemed to lick up the surges of the stream; but Sam, snugly sheltered under rock and tree, lay crouching in his skiff, rocking upon the billows until he fell asleep. When he awoke all was quiet. The gust had passed away, and only now and then a faint gleam of lightning in the east showed which way it had gone. The night was dark and moonless; and from the state of the tide Sam concluded it was near midnight. He was on the point of making loose his skiff to return homewards, when he saw a light gleaming along the water from a distance, which seemed rapidly approaching. As it drew near he perceived it came from a lantern in the bow of a boat gliding along under the shadow of the land. It pulled up in a small cove, close to where he was. A man jumped on shore, and searching about with the lantern, exclaimed, " This is the place — here's the iron ring." The boat was then made fast, and the man returning on board, assisted his comrades in conveying something heavy on shore. As the light gleamed among them, Sam saw that they were five stout desperate-looking fellows, in red woollen caps, with a leader in a three-cornered hat, and that some of them were armed with dirks, or long knives, and pistols. They talked low to one another, and occasionally in some outlandish tongue which he could not understand.

On landing they made their way among the bushes, taking turns to relieve each other in lugging their burden up the rocky bank. Sam's curiosity was now fully aroused; so leaving his skiff he clambered silently up a ridge that overlooked their path. They had stopped to rest for a moment, and the leader was looking about among the bushes with his lantern. " Have you brought the spades? " said one. " They are here," replied another, who had them on his shoulder. " We must dig deep, where there will be no risk of discovery," said a third.

A cold chill ran through Sam's veins. He fancied he saw before him a gang of murderers, about to bury their victim. His knees smote together. In his agitation he shook the branch of a tree with which he was supporting himself as he looked over the edge of the cliff.

" What's that? " cried one of the gang. — " Some one stirs among the bushes! "

The lantern was held up in the direction of the noise. One of the red-caps cocked a pistol, and pointed it towards the very place where Sam was standing. He stood motionless — breathless; expecting the next moment to be his last. Fortunately his dingy complexion was in his favor, and made no glare among the leaves.

" 'Tis no one," said the man with the lantern. " What a plague! you would not fire off your pistol and alarm the country! "

The pistol was uncocked; the burden was resumed, and the party slowly toiled along the bank. Sam watched them as

they went; the light sending back fitful gleams through the
dripping bushes, and it was not until they were fairly out of
sight that he ventured to draw breath freely. He now thought
of getting back to his boat, and making his escape out of the
reach of such dangerous neighbors; but curiosity was all-
powerful. He hesitated and lingered and listened. By and by
he heard the strokes of spades. — "They are digging the
grave!" said he to himself; and the cold sweat started upon his
forehead. Every stroke of a spade, as it sounded through the
silent groves, went to his heart; it was evident there was as little
noise made as possible; everything had an air of terrible mystery and secrecy. Sam had a great relish for the horrible, — a
tale of murder was a treat for him; and he was a constant attendant at executions. He could not resist an impulse, in spite
of every danger, to steal nearer to the scene of mystery, and
overlook the midnight fellows at their work. He crawled along
cautiously, therefore, inch by inch; stepping with the utmost

care among the dry leaves, lest their rustling should betray him. He came at length to where a steep rock intervened between him and the gang; for he saw the light of their lantern shining up against the branches of the trees on the other side. Sam slowly and silently clambered up the surface of the rock, and raising his head above its naked edge, beheld the villains immediately below him, and so near, that though he dreaded discovery, he dared not withdraw lest the least movement should be heard. In this way he remained, with his round black face peering above the edge of the rock, like the sun just emerging above the edge of the horizon, or the round-cheeked moon on the dial of a clock.

The red-caps had nearly finished their work; the grave was filled up, and they were carefully replacing the turf. This done, they scattered dry leaves over the place. "And now," said the leader, "I defy the devil himself to find it out."

"The murderers!" exclaimed Sam, involuntarily.

The whole gang started, and looking up, beheld the round black head of Sam just above them. His white eyes strained half out of their orbits; his white teeth chattering, and his whole visage shining with cold perspiration.

" We're discovered! " cried one.

" Down with him! " cried another.

Sam heard the cocking of a pistol, but did not pause for the report. He scrambled over rock and stone, through brush and brier; rolled down banks like a hedge-hog; scrambled up others like a catamount. In every direction he heard some one or other of the gang hemming him in. At length he reached the rocky ridge along the river; one of the red-caps was hard behind him. A steep rock like a wall rose directly in his way; it seemed to cut off all retreat, when fortunately he espied the strong cord-like branch of a grape-vine reaching half-way down it. He sprang at it with the force of a desperate man, seized it with both hands, and being young and agile, succeeded in swinging himself to the summit of the cliff. Here he stood in full relief against the sky, when the red-cap cocked his pistol and fired. The ball whistled by Sam's head. With the lucky thought of a man in an emergency, he uttered a yell, fell to the ground, and detached at the same time a fragment of the rock, which tumbled with a loud splash into the river.

" I've done his business," said the red-cap to one or two of his comrades as they arrived panting. " He'll tell no tales, except to the fishes in the river."

His pursuers now turned to meet their companions. Sam, sliding silently down the surface of the rock, let himself quietly into his skiff, cast loose the fastening, and abandoned himself to the rapid current, which in that place runs like a mill-

stream, and soon swept him off from the neighborhood. It was not, however, until he had drifted a great distance that he ventured to ply his oars, when he made his skiff dart like an arrow through the strait of Hell Gate, never heeding the danger of Pot, Frying-Pan, nor Hog's Back itself: nor did he feel himself thoroughly secure until safely nestled in bed in the cockloft of the ancient farm-house of the Suydams.

Here the worthy Peechy Prauw paused to take breath, and to take a sip of the gossip tankard that stood at his elbow. His auditors remained with open mouths and outstretched necks, gaping like a nest of swallows for an additional mouthful.

" And is that all? " exclaimed the half-pay officer.

" That's all that belongs to the story," said Peechy Prauw.

" And did Sam never find out what was buried by the red-caps? " said Wolfert, eagerly, whose mind was haunted by nothing but ingots and doubloons.

" Not that I know of," said Peechy; " he had no time to spare from his work, and, to tell the truth, he did not like to run the risk of another race among the rocks. Besides, how should he recollect the spot where the grave had been digged? everything would look so different by daylight. And then, where was the use of looking for a dead body, when there was no chance of hanging the murderers? "

" Aye, but are you sure it was a dead body they buried? " said Wolfert.

" To be sure," cried Peechy Prauw, exultingly. " Does it not haunt the neighborhood to this very day? "

"Haunts!" exclaimed several of the party, opening their eyes still wider, and edging their chairs still closer.

"Aye, haunts," repeated Peechy; "have none of you heard of Father Red-cap, who haunts the old burnt farm-house in the woods, on the border of the Sound, near Hell Gate? That farm-house stands hard by the very spot. It's been unoccupied time out of mind, and stands in a lonely part of the coast; but those who fish in the neighborhood have often heard strange noises there; and lights have been seen about the wood at night; and an old fellow in a red cap has been seen at the windows more than once, which people take to be the ghost of the body buried there. Once upon a time three soldiers took shelter in the building for the night, and rummaged it from top to bottom, when they found old Father Red-cap astride of a cider-barrel in the cellar, with a jug in one hand and a goblet in the other. He offered them a drink out of his goblet, but just as one of the soldiers was putting it to his mouth — whew! — a flash of fire blazed through the cellar, blinded every mother's son of them for several minutes, when they recovered their eye-sight, jug, goblet, and Red-cap had vanished, and nothing but the empty cider-barrel remained."

Here the half-pay officer, who was growing very muzzy and sleepy, and nodding over his liquor, with half-extinguished eye, suddenly gleamed up like an expiring rushlight.

"That's all fudge!" said he, as Peechy finished his last story.

"Well, I don't vouch for the truth of it myself," said Peechy Prauw, "though all the world knows that there's something strange about that house and grounds; but as to the story of Mud Sam, I believe it just as well as if it had happened to myself."

The deep interest taken in this conversation by the company had made them unconscious of the uproar abroad among the elements, when suddenly they were electrified by a tremendous clap of thunder. A lumbering crash followed instantaneously, shaking the building to its very foundation. All started from their seats, imagining it the shock of an earthquake, or that old Father Red-cap was coming among them in all his terrors. They listened for a moment, but only heard the rain pelting against the windows, and the wind howling among the trees. The explosion was soon explained by the apparition of an old negro's bald head thrust in at the door, his white goggle eyes contrasting with his jetty poll, which was wet with rain, and shone like a bottle. In a jargon but half intelligible, he announced that the kitchen-chimney had been struck with lightning.

A sullen pause of the storm, which now rose and sunk in gusts, produced a momentary stillness. In this interval the report of a musket was heard, and a long shout, almost like a yell, resounded from the shores. Every one crowded to the window; another musket-shot was heard, and another long shout, mingled wildly with a rising blast of wind. It seemed as if the cry came up from the bosom of the waters; for though incessant flashes of lightning spread a light about the shore, no one was to be seen.

Suddenly the window of the room overhead was opened,

and a loud halloo uttered by the mysterious stranger. Several hailings passed from one party to the other, but in a language which none of the company in the bar-room could understand; and presently they heard the window closed, and a great noise overhead, as if all the furniture were pulled and hauled about the room. The negro servant was summoned, and shortly afterwards was seen assisting the veteran to lug the ponderous sea-chest downstairs.

The landlord was in amazement. " What, you are not going on the water in such a storm? "

" Storm! " said the other, scornfully, " do you call such a sputter of weather a storm? "

" You'll get drenched to the skin, — you'll catch your death! " said Peechy Prauw, affectionately.

" Thunder and lightning! " exclaimed the veteran, " don't preach about weather to a man that has cruised in whirlwinds and tornadoes."

The obsequious Peechy was again struck dumb. The voice from the water was heard once more in a tone of impatience; the by-standers stared with redoubled awe at this man of storms, who seemed to have come up out of the deep, and to be summoned back to it again.

As, with the assistance of the negro, he slowly bore his ponderous sea-chest towards the shore, they eyed it with a superstitious feeling, — half doubting whether he were not really about to embark upon it and launch forth upon the wild waves. They followed him at a distance with a lantern.

"Dowse the light!" roared the hoarse voice from the water. "No one wants light here!"

"Thunder and lightning!' exclaimed the veteran, turning short upon them; "back to the house with you!"

Wolfert and his companions shrunk back in dismay. Still their curiosity would not allow them entirely to withdraw. A long sheet of lightning now flickered across the waves, and discovered a boat, filled with men, just under a rocky point, rising and sinking with the heaving surges, and swashing the waters at every heave. It was with difficulty held to the rocks by a boat-hook, for the current rushed furiously round the point. The veteran hoisted one end of the lumbering sea-chest on the gunwale of the boat, and seized the handle at the other end to lift it in, when the motion propelled the boat from the shore; the chest slipped off from the gunwale, and, sinking into the waves, pulled the veteran headlong after it. A loud shriek was uttered by all on shore, and a volley of execrations by those on board; but boat and man were hurried away by the rushing swiftness of the tide. A pitchy darkness succeeded; Wolfert Webber indeed fancied that he distinguished a cry for help, and that he beheld the drowning man beckoning for assistance; but when the lightning again gleamed along the water, all was void; neither man nor boat was to be seen; nothing but the dashing and weltering of the waves as they hurried past.

The company returned to the tavern to await the subsiding of the storm. They resumed their seats, and gazed on each other with dismay. The whole transaction had not occupied five minutes, and not a dozen words had been spoken. When they looked at the oaken chair, they could scarcely realize the fact that the strange being who had so lately tenanted it, full of life and Herculean vigor, should already be a corpse. There was the very glass he had just drunk from; there lay the ashes from the pipe which he had smoked, as it were, with his last breath. As the worthy burghers pondered on these things, they felt a terrible conviction of the uncertainty of existence, and each felt as if the ground on which he stood was rendered less stable by his awful example.

The landlord was particularly happy that the poor dear man had paid his reckoning before he went; and made a kind of farewell speech on the occasion.

" He came," said he, " in a storm, and he went in a storm; he came in the night, and he went in the night; he came nobody knows whence, and he has gone nobody knows where. For aught I know he has gone to sea once more on his chest, and may land to bother some people on the other side of the world! Though it's a thousand pities," added he, " if he has gone to Davy Jones's locker that he had not left his own locker behind him."

" His locker! St. Nicholas preserve us! " cried Peechy Prauw. " I'd not have had that sea-chest in the house for any money; I'll warrant he'd come racketing after it at nights, and making a haunted house of the inn. And, as to his going to sea in his chest, I recollect what happened to Skipper Onderdonk's ship on his voyage from Amsterdam.

" The boatswain died during a storm: so they wrapped him up in a sheet, and put him in his own sea-chest, and threw him overboard; but they neglected in their hurry-skurry to say prayers over him — and the storm raged and roared louder than ever, and they saw the dead man seated in his chest, with his shroud for a sail, coming hard after the ship; and the sea breaking before him in great sprays like fire; and there they kept scudding day after day, and night after night, expecting every moment to go to wreck: and every night they saw the dead boatswain in his sea-chest trying to get up with them, and they heard his whistle above the blasts of wind, and he seemed to send great seas mountain-high after them, that would have swamped the ship if they had not put up the dead-lights. And so it went on till they lost sight of him in the fogs off Newfoundland, and supposed he had veered ship and stood for Dead Man's Isle. So much for burying a man at sea without saying prayers over him."

Wolfert Webber now carried home a fresh stock of stories and notions to ruminate upon. These accounts of pots of money and Spanish treasures, buried here and there and everywhere, about the rocks and bays of these wild shores, made him almost dizzy. "Blessed St. Nicholas!" ejaculated he, half aloud, "is it not possible to come upon one of the golden hoards, and to make one's self rich in a twinkling? How hard that I must go on delving and delving, day in and day out, merely to make a morsel of bread, when one lucky stroke of a spade might enable me to ride in my carriage for the rest of my life!"

As he turned over in his thoughts all that had been told of the singular adventure of the negro fisherman, his imagination gave a totally different complexion to the tale. He saw in the gang of red-caps nothing but a crew of pirates burying their spoils, and his cupidity was once more awakened by the possibility of at length getting on the traces of some of this lurking wealth. Indeed, his infected fancy tinged everything with gold. He felt like the greedy inhabitant of Bagdad, when his eyes had been greased with the magic ointment of the dervise, that gave him to see all the treasures of the earth. Caskets of buried jewels, chests of ingots, and barrels of outlandish coins, seemed to court him from their concealments, and supplicate him to relieve them from their untimely graves.

On making private inquiries about the grounds said to be haunted by Father Red-cap, he was more and more confirmed in his surmise. He learned that the place had several times been visited by experienced money-diggers, who had heard Black Sam's story, though none of them had met with success. On the contrary, they had always been dogged with ill-luck of some kind or other, in consequence, as Wolfert concluded, of not going to work at the proper time, and with the proper ceremonials. The last attempt had been made by Cobus Quackenbos, who dug for a whole night, and met with incredible difficulty, for as fast as he threw one shovelful of earth out of the hole, two were thrown in by invisible hands. He succeeded so far, however, as to uncover an iron chest, when there was a terrible roaring, ramping, and raging of uncouth figures about the hole, and at length a shower of blows, dealt by invisible cudgels, fairly belabored him off the forbidden ground. This Cobus Quackenbos had declared on his death-bed, so that there could not be any doubt of it. He was a man that had devoted many years of his life to money-digging, and it was thought would have ultimately succeeded, had he not died recently of a brain-fever in the almshouse.

Wolfert Webber was now in a worry of trepidation and impatience; fearful lest some rival adventurer should get a scene of the buried gold. He determined privately to seek out the black fisherman, and get him to serve as guide to the place where he had witnessed the mysterious scene of interment. Sam was easily found; for he was one of those old habitual beings that live about a neighborhood until they wear themselves a place in the public mind, and become, in a manner, public characters. There was not an unlucky urchin about town that did not know Sam the fisherman, and think that he had a right to play his tricks upon the old negro. Sam had led an amphibious life for more than half a century, about the shores of the bay, and the fishing-grounds of the Sound. He passed the greater part of his time on and in the water, particularly about Hell Gate; and might have been taken, in bad weather, for one of the hobgoblins that used to haunt that strait. There would he be seen, at all times, and in all weathers; sometimes in his skiff, anchored among the eddies, or prowling like a shark about some wreck, where the fish are supposed to be most abundant. Sometimes seated on a rock from hour to hour, looking, in the mist and drizzle, like a solitary heron watching for its prey. He was well acquainted with every hole and corner of the Sound; from the Wallabout to Hell Gate, and from Hell Gate unto the Devil's Stepping-Stones; and it was even affirmed that he knew all the fish in the river by their Christian names.

Wolfert found him at his cabin, which was not much larger than a tolerable dog-house. It was rudely constructed of fragments of wrecks and drift-wood, and built on the rocky shore, at the root of the old fort, just about what at present forms the point of the Battery. A most ancient and fishlike smell pervaded the place. Oars, paddles, and fishing-rods were leaning against the wall of the fort; a net was spread on the sand to dry; a skiff was drawn up on the beach; and at the door of his cabin was Mud Sam himself, indulging in the true negro luxury of sleeping in the sunshine.

Many years had passed away since the time of Sam's youthful adventure, and the snows of many a winter had grizzled the knotty wool upon his head. He perfectly recollected the circumstances, however, for he had often been called upon to relate them. As to the subsequent researches of money-diggers, Sam knew nothing about them; they were matters quite out of his line; neither did the cautious Wolfert care to disturb his thoughts on that point. His only wish was to secure the old fisherman as a pilot to the spot; and this was readily effected. The long time that had intervened since his nocturnal adventure had effaced all Sam's awe of the place, and the promise of a trifling reward roused him at once from his sleep and his sunshine.

The tide was adverse to making the expedition by water, and Wolfert was too impatient to get to the land of promise to wait for its turning; they set off, therefore, by land. A walk of four or five miles brought them to the edge of the wood, which at that time covered the greater part of the eastern side of the island. It was just beyond the pleasant region of Bloomen-dael. Here they stuck into a long lane, straggling among trees and bushes, very much overgrown with weeds and mullein-stalks, as if but seldom used, and so completely overshadowed as to enjoy but a kind of twilight. Wild vines entangled the trees and flaunted in their faces; brambles and briers caught their clothes as they passed; the garter-snake glided across their path; the spotted toad hopped and waddled before them, and the restless cat-bird mewed at them from every thicket.

On reaching the lower end of the lane, they found themselves near the shore of the Sound in a kind of amphitheatre, surrounded by forest-trees. The area had once been a grass-plot, but was now shagged with briers and rank weeds. At one end, and just on the river bank, was a ruined building, little better than a heap of rubbish, with a stack of chimneys rising like a solitary tower out of the centre. The current of the Sound rushed along just below it; with wildly grown trees drooping their branches into its waves.

Wolfert had not a doubt that this was the haunted house of Father Red-cap. The evening was approaching, and the light falling dubiously among the woody places, gave a melancholy tone to the scene, well calculated to foster any lurking feeling of awe or superstition. The night-hawk, wheeling about in the highest regions of the air, emitted his peevish, boding cry. The woodpecker gave a lonely tap now and then on some hollow tree, and the fire-bird[1] streamed by them with his deep-red plumage.

[1] Orchard oriole.

They now came to an enclosure that had once been a garden. It extended along the foot of a rocky ridge, but was little better than a wilderness of weeds, with here and there a matted rose-bush, or a peach or plum tree grown wild and ragged and covered with moss. At the lower end of the garden they passed a kind of vault in the side of a bank, facing the water. It had the look of a root-house. The door, though decayed, was still strong, and appeared to have been recently patched up. Wolfert pushed it open. It gave a harsh grating upon its hinges, and striking against something like a box, a rattling sound ensued, and a skull rolled on the floor. Wolfert drew back shuddering, but was reassured on being informed by the negro that this was a family vault, belonging to one of the old Dutch families that owned this estate; an assertion corroborated by the sight of coffins of various sizes piled within. Sam had been familiar with all these scenes when a boy, and now knew that he could not be far from the place of which they were in quest.

They made their way to the water's edge, scrambling along ledges of rocks that overhung the waves, and obliged often to hold by shrubs and grape-vines to avoid slipping into the deep and hurried stream. At length they came to a small cove. It was protected by steep rocks, and overshadowed by a thick copse of oaks and chestnuts. The beach shelved gradually within the cove, but the current swept deep, and black, and rapid, along its jutting points. The negro paused, raised his remnant of a hat, and scratched his grizzled poll for a moment, as he regarded this nook; then suddenly clapping his hands, he stepped exultingly forward, and pointed to a large iron ring, stapled firmly in the rock, just where a broad shelf of stone furnished a commodious landing-place. It was the very spot where the red-caps had landed. Years had changed the more perishable features of the scene; but rock and iron yield slowly to the influence of time. On looking more closely, Wolfert remarked three crosses cut in the rock just above the ring, which had no doubt some mysterious signification. Old Sam now readily recognized the overhanging rock under which his skiff had been sheltered during the thunder-gust. To follow up the course which the midnight gang had taken, however, was a harder task. His mind had been so much taken up on that eventful occasion by the persons of the drama, as to pay but little attention to the scenes; and these places look so different by night and day. After wandering about for some time, however, they came to an opening among the trees which Sam thought resembled the place. There was a ledge of rock of moderate height like a wall on one side, which he thought might be the very ridge whence he had overlooked the diggers. Wolfert examined it narrowly, and at length discovered three crosses similar to those on the above ring, cut deeply into the face of the rock, but nearly obliterated by moss that had grown over them. His heart leaped with joy, for he doubted not they were the private marks of the buccaneers. All now that remained was to ascertain the precise spot where the treasure lay buried; for otherwise he might dig at random in the neighborhood of the crosses, without coming upon the spoils, and he had already had enough of such profitless labor. Here, however, the old negro was perfectly at a loss, and indeed perplexed him by a variety of opinions; for his recollections were all confused. Sometimes he declared it must have been at the foot of a mulberry-tree hard by; then beside a great white stone; then under a small green knoll, a short distance from the ledge of rocks; until at length Wolfert became as bewildered as himself.

The shadows of evening were now spreading themselves over the woods, and rock and tree began to mingle together. It was evidently too late to attempt anything further at present; and, indeed, Wolfert had come unprovided with implements to prosecute his researches. Satisfied, therefore, with having ascertained the place, he took note of all its landmarks, that he might recognize it again, and set out on his return homewards, resolved to prosecute this golden enterprise without delay.

Their way back lay through the desolate garden, and Wolfert's nerves had arrived at so sensitive a state that the flitting of a bird, the rustling of a leaf, or the falling of a nut, was enough to startle him. As they entered the confines of the garden, they caught sight of a figure at a distance advancing slowly up one of the walks, and bending under the weight of a burden. They paused and regarded him attentively. He wore what appeared to be a woollen cap, still more alarming, of a most sanguinary red.

The figure moved slowly on, ascended the bank, and stopped at the very door of the sepulchral vault. Just before entering it he looked around. What was the affright of Wolfert when he recognized the grizzly visage of the drowned buccaneer! He uttered an ejaculation of horror. The figure slowly raised his iron fist, and shook it with a terrible menace. Wolfert

105

did not pause to see any more, but hurried off as fast as his legs could carry him, nor was Sam slow in following at his heels, having all his ancient terrors revived. Away, then, did they scramble through bush and brake, horribly frightened at every bramble that tugged at their skirts, nor did they pause to breathe, until they had blundered their way through this perilous wood, and fairly reached the high-road to the city.

Several days elapsed before Wolfert could summon courage enough to prosecute the enterprise, so much had he been dismayed by the apparition, whether living or dead, of the grisly buccaneer. In the meantime, what a conflict of mind did he suffer! He neglected all his concerns, was moody and restless all day, lost his appetite, wandered in his thoughts and words, and committed a thousand blunders. His rest was broken; and when he fell asleep, the nightmare, in shape of a huge money-bag, sat squatted upon his breast. He babbled about incalculable sums; fancied himself engaged in money-digging; threw the bedclothes right and left, in the idea that he was shovelling away the dirt; groped under the bed in quest of the treasure, and lugged forth, as he supposed, an inestimable pot of gold.

Dame Webber and her daughter were in despair at what they conceived a returning touch of insanity. There are two family oracles, one or other of which Dutch housewives consult in all cases of great doubt and perplexity — the dominie and the doctor. In the present instance they repaired to the doctor. There was at that time a little dark mouldy man of medicine, famous among the old wives of the Manhattoes for his skill, not only in the healing art, but in all matters of strange and mysterious nature. His name was Dr. Knipperhausen, but he was more commonly known by the appellation of the High-German Doctor. To him did the poor woman repair for counsel and assistance touching the mental vagaries of Wolfert Webber.

They found the doctor seated in his little study, clad in his dark camlet robe of knowledge, with his black velvet cap; after the manner of Boerhaave, Van Helmont, and other medical sages; a pair of green spectacles set in black horn upon his clubbed nose, and poring over a German folio that reflected back the darkness of his physiognomy. The doctor listened to their statement of the symptoms of Wolfert's malady with profound attention; but when they came to mention his raving about buried money, the little man pricked up his ears.

Dr. Knipperhausen had been half his life engaged in seeking the short cuts to fortune, in quest of which so many a long lifetime is wasted. He had passed some years of his youth among the Harz mountains of Germany, and had derived much valuable instruction from the miners, touching the mode of seeking treasure buried in the earth. He had prosecuted his studies also under a travelling sage who united the mysteries of medicine with magic and legerdemain. His mind therefore had become stored with all kinds of mystic lore: he had dabbled a little in astrology, alchemy, divination; knew how to detect stolen money, and to tell where springs of water lay hidden; in a word, by the dark nature of his knowledge he had acquired the name of the High-German Doctor, which is pretty nearly equivalent to that of necromancer. The doctor had often heard rumors of treasure being buried in various parts of the island,

and had long been anxious to get on the traces of it. No sooner were Wolfert's waking and sleeping vagaries confided to him, than he beheld in them the confirmed symptoms of a case of money-digging, and lost no time in probing it to the bottom. Wolfert had long been sorely oppressed in mind by the golden secret, and as a family physician is a kind of father confessor, he was glad of any opportunity of unburdening himself. So far from curing, the doctor caught the malady from his patient. The circumstances unfolded to him awakened all his cupidity: he had not a doubt of money being buried somewhere in the neighborhood of the mysterious crosses, and offered to join Wolfert in the search. He informed him that much secrecy and caution must be observed in enterprises of that kind; that money is only to be digged for at night; with certain forms and ceremonies, and burning of drugs, the repeating of mystic words; and above all, that the seekers must first be provided with a divining rod, which had the wonderful property of pointing to the very spot on the surface of the earth under which treasure lay hidden. As the doctor had given much of his mind to these matters, he charged himself with all the necessary preparations, and, as the quarter of the moon was propitious, he undertook to have the divining rod ready by a certain night.

Wolfert's heart leaped with joy at having met with so learned and able a coadjutor. Everything went on secretly, but swimmingly. The doctor had many consultations with his patient, and the good woman of the household lauded the comforting effect of his visits. In the meantime the wonderful divining rod, that great key to nature's secrets, was duly prepared.

The doctor had thumbed over all his books of knowledge for the occasion; and the black fisherman was engaged to take them in his skiff to the scene of enterprise; to work with spade and pickaxe in unearthing the treasure; and to freight his bark with the weighty spoils they were certain of finding.

At length the appointed night arrived for this perilous undertaking. Before Wolfert left his home he counselled his wife and daughter to go to bed, and feel no alarm if he should not return during the night. Like reasonable women, on being told not to feel alarm they fell immediately into a panic. They saw at once by his manner that something unusual was in agitation; all their fears about the unsettled state of his mind were revived with tenfold force: they hung about him, entreating him not to expose himself to the night air, but all in vain. When once Wolfert was mounted on his hobby, it was no easy matter to get him out of the saddle. It was a clear starlight night, when he issued out of the portal of the Webber palace. He wore a large flapped hat tied under the chin with a handkerchief of his daughter's, to secure him from the night damp, while Dame Webber threw her long red cloak about his shoulders, and fastened it round his neck.

The doctor had been no less carefully armed and accoutred by his housekeeper, the vigilant Frau Ilsy; and sallied forth in his camlet robe by way of surcoat; his black velvet cap under his cocked hat, a thick clasped book under his arm, a basket of drugs and dried herbs in one hand, and in the other the miraculous rod of divination.

The great church-clock struck ten as Wolfert and the doctor passed by the churchyard, and the watchman bawled in a hoarse voice a long and doleful " All's well! " A deep sleep had already fallen upon this primitive burgh: nothing disturbed this awful silence, excepting now and then the bark of some poor profligate night-walking dog, or the serenade of some romantic cat. It is true, Wolfert fancied more than once that he heard the sound of a stealthy footfall at a distance behind them; but it might have been merely the echo of their own steps along the quiet streets. He thought also at one time that he saw a tall figure skulking after them — stopping when they stopped, and moving on as they proceeded; but the dim and uncertain lamp-light threw such vague gleams and shadows, that this might all have been mere fancy.

They found the old fisherman waiting for them, smoking his pipe in the stern of the skiff, which was moored just in front of his little cabin. A pickaxe and spade were lying in the bottom of the boat, with a dark lantern, and a stone bottle of good Dutch courage, in which honest Sam no doubt put even more faith than Dr. Knipperhausen in his drugs.

Thus then did these three worthies embark in their cockleshell of a skiff upon this nocturnal expedition, with a wisdom and valor equalled only by the three wise men of Gotham, who adventured to sea in a bowl. The tide was rising and running rapidly up the Sound. The current bore them along, almost without the aid of an oar. The profile of the town lay all in shadow. Here and there a light feebly glimmered from some sick-chamber, or from the cabin-window of some vessel at anchor in the stream. Not a cloud obscured the deep starry firmament, the lights of which wavered on the surface of the placid river; and a shooting meteor, streaking its pale course in the very direction they were taking, was interpreted by the doctor into a most propitious omen.

In a little while they glided by the point of Corlaer's Hook with the rural inn which had been the scene of such night adventures. The family had retired to rest, and the house was dark and still. Wolfert felt a chill pass over him as they passed the point where the buccaneer had disappeared. He pointed it out to Dr. Knipperhausen. While regarding it, they thought they saw a boat actually lurking at the very place, but the shore cast such a shadow over the border of the water that they could discern nothing distinctly. They had not proceeded far when they heard the low sounds of distant oars, as if cautiously pulled. Sam plied his oars with redoubled vigor, and knowing all the eddies and currents of the stream, soon left their followers, if such they were, far astern. In a little while they stretched across Turtle Bay and Kip's Bay, then shrouded themselves in the deep shadows of Manhattan shore, and glided swiftly along, secure from observation. At length the negro shot his skiff into a little cove, darkly embowered by trees, and made it fast to the well-known iron ring. They now landed, and lighting the lantern, gathered their various implements and proceeded slowly through the bushes. Every sound startled them, even that of their own footsteps among the dry leaves; and the hooting of a screech-owl, from the shattered chimney of the neighboring ruin, made their blood run cold.

In spite of all Wolfert's caution in taking note of the landmarks, it was some time before they could find the open place among the trees, where the treasure was supposed to be buried. At length they came to the ledge of rock; and on examining its surface by the aid of the lantern, Wolfert recognized the three mystic crosses. Their hearts beat quick, for the momentous trial was at hand that was to determine their hopes.

The lantern was now held by Wolfert Webber, while the doctor produced the divining rod. It was a forked twig, one end of which was grasped firmly in each hand, while the centre, forming the stem, pointed perpendicularly upwards. The doctor moved this wand about, within a certain distance of the earth, from place to place, but for some time without any effect, while Wolfert kept the light of the lantern turned full upon it, and watched it with the most breathless interest. At length the rod began slowly to turn. The doctor grasped it with greater earnestness, his hands trembling with the agitation of his mind. The wand continued to turn gradually, until at length the stem had reversed its position, and pointed perpendicularly downward, and remained pointing to one spot as fixedly as the needle to the pole.

"This is the spot!" said the doctor, in an almost inaudible tone.

Wolfert's heart was in his throat.

113

" Shall I dig? " said the negro, grasping the spade.

" *Pots tausend,* no! " replied the little doctor, hastily. He now ordered his companions to keep close by him, and to maintain the most inflexible silence. That certain precautions must be taken and ceremonies used to prevent the evil spirits which kept about buried treasure from doing them any harm. He then drew a circle about the place, enough to include the whole party. He next gathered dry twigs and leaves and made a fire, upon which he threw certain drugs and dried herbs which he had brought in his basket. A thick smoke rose, diffusing a potent odor, savoring marvellously of brimstone and assafœtida, which, however grateful it might be to the olfactory nerves of spirits, nearly strangled poor Wolfert, and produced a fit of coughing and wheezing that made the whole grove resound. Dr. Knipperhausen then unclasped the volume which he had brought under his arm, which was printed in red and black characters in German text. While Wolfert held the lantern, the doctor, by the aid of his spectacles, read off several forms of conjuration in Latin and German. He then ordered Sam to seize the pickaxe and proceed to work. The close-bound soil gave obstinate signs of not having been disturbed for many a year. After having picked his way through the surface, Sam came to a bed of sand and gravel, which he threw briskly to right and left with the spade.

" Hark! " said Wolfert, who fancied he heard a trampling among the dry leaves, and a rustling through the bushes. Sam paused for a moment, and they listened. No footstep was near. The bat flitted by them in silence; a bird, roused from its roost by the light which glared up among the trees, flew circling about the flame. In the profound stillness of the woodland, they could distinguish the current rippling along the rocky shore, and the distant murmuring and roaring of Hell Gate.

The negro continued his labors, and had already digged a considerable hole. The doctor stood on the edge, reading formulæ every now and then from his black-letter volume, or throwing more drugs and herbs upon the fire; while Wolfert bent anxiously over the pit, watching every stroke of the spade. Any one witnessing the scene thus lighted up by fire, lantern, and the reflection of Wolfert's red mantle, might have mistaken the little doctor for some foul magician, busied in his incantations, and the grizzly-headed negro for some swart goblin, obedient to his commands.

At length the spade of the fisherman struck upon something that sounded hollow. The sound vibrated to Wolfert's heart. He struck his spade again. —

" 'Tis a chest," said Sam.

" Full of gold, I'll warrant it! " cried Wolfert.

Scarcely had he uttered the words when a sound from above caught his ear. He cast up his eyes, and lo! by the expiring light of the fire he beheld, just over the disk of the rock, what appeared to be the grim visage of the drowned buccaneer, grinning hideously down upon him.

Wolfert gave a loud cry, and let fall the lantern. His panic communicated itself to his companions. The negro leaped out of the hole; the doctor dropped his book and basket, and began to pray in German. All was horror and confusion. The fire

was scattered about, the lantern extinguished. In their hurry-
scurry they ran against and confounded one another. They fancied a legion of hobgoblins let loose upon them, and that they
saw, by the fitful gleams of the scattered embers, strange figures, in red caps, gibbering and ramping around them. The
doctor ran one way, the negro another, and Wolfert made for
the water side. As he plunged struggling onwards through
brush and brake, he heard the tread of some one in pursuit. He
scrambled frantically forward. The footsteps gained upon him.
He felt himself grasped by his cloak, when suddenly his pursuer was attacked in turn: a fierce fight and struggle ensued —
a pistol was discharged that lit up rock and bush for a second,
and showed two figures grappling together — all was then
darker than ever. The contest continued — the combatants
clinched each other, and panted and groaned, and rolled among
the rocks. There was snarling and growling as of a cur, mingled with curses, in which Wolfert fancied he could recognize
the voice of the buccaneer. He would fain have fled, but he was
on the brink of a precipice, and could go no farther.

Again the parties were on their feet; again there was a
tugging and struggling, as if strength alone could decide the
combat, until one was precipitated from the brow of the cliff,
and sent headlong into the deep stream that whirled below.
Wolfert heard the plunge, and a kind of strangling, bubbling
murmur, but the darkness of the night hid everything from him,
and the swiftness of the current swept everything instantly out
of hearing. One of the combatants was disposed of, but whether
friend or foe, Wolfert could not tell, nor whether they might

not both be foes. He heard the survivor approach, and his terror revived. He saw, where the profile of the rocks rose against the horizon, a human form advancing. He could not be mistaken: it must be the buccaneer. Whither should he fly! — a precipice was on one side — a murderer on the other. The enemy approached — he was close at hand. Wolfert attempted to let himself down the face of the cliff. His cloak caught in a thorn that grew on the edge. He was jerked from off his feet, and held dangling in the air, half-choked by the string with which his careful wife had fastened the garment around his neck. Wolfert thought his last moment was arrived; already had he committed his soul to St. Nicholas, when the string broke, and he tumbled down the bank, bumping from rock to rock, and bush to bush, and leaving the red cloak fluttering like a bloody banner in the air.

It was a long while before Wolfert came to himself. When he opened his eyes, the ruddy streaks of morning were already shooting up the sky. He found himself grievously battered, and lying in the bottom of a boat. He attempted to sit up, but was too sore and stiff to move. A voice requested him in friendly accents to lie still. He turned his eyes towards the speaker: it was Dirk Waldron. He had dogged the party, at the earnest request of Dame Webber and her daughter, who, with the laudable curiosity of their sex, had pried into the secret consultations of Wolfert and the doctor. Dirk had been completely distanced in following the light skiff of the fisherman, and had just come in to rescue the poor money-digger from his pursuer.

Thus ended this perilous enterprise. The doctor and Black Sam severally found their way back to the Manhattoes, each having some dreadful tale of peril to relate. As to poor Wolfert, instead of returning in triumph laden with bags of gold, he was borne home on a shutter, followed by a rabble-rout of curious urchins. His wife and daughter saw the dismal pageant from a distance, and alarmed the neighborhood with their cries; they thought the poor man had suddenly settled the great debt of nature in one of his wayward moods. Finding him, however, still living, they had him speedily to bed, and a jury of old matrons of the neighborhood assembled, to determine how he should be doctored. The whole town was in a buzz with the story of the money-diggers. Many repaired to the scene of the previous night's adventures: but though they found the very place of the digging, they discovered nothing that compensated them for their trouble. Some say they found the fragments of an oaken chest, and an iron pot-lid, which savored strongly of hidden money; and that in the old family

119

vault there were traces of bales and boxes: but this is all very dubious.

In fact, the secret of all this story has never to this day been discovered: whether any treasure were ever actually buried at that place; whether, if so, it were carried off at night by those who had buried it; or whether it still remains there under the guardianship of gnomes and spirits until it shall be properly sought for, is all matter of conjecture. For my part, I incline to the latter opinion; and make no doubt that great sums lie buried, both there and in other parts of this island and its neighborhood, ever since the times of the buccaneers and the Dutch colonists; and I would earnestly recommend the search after them to such of my fellow-citizens as are not engaged in any other speculations.

There were many conjectures formed, also, as to who and what was the strange man of the seas who had domineered over the little fraternity at Corlaer's Hook for a time, disappeared so strangely, and reappeared so fearfully.

Some supposed him a smuggler stationed at that place to assist his comrades in landing their goods among the rocky coves of the island. Others, that he was one of the ancient comrades of Kidd or Bradish, returned to convey away treasures formerly hidden in the vicinity. The only circumstance that throws anything like a vague light on this mysterious matter, is a report which prevailed of a strange foreign-built shallop, with much the look of a picaroon, having been seen hovering about the Sound for several days without landing or reporting herself, though boats were seen going to and from her at night;

and that she was seen standing out of the mouth of the harbor, in the gray of the dawn, after the catastrophe of the money-diggers.

I must not omit to mention another report, also, of the buccaneer, who was supposed to have been drowned, being seen before daybreak, with a lantern in his hand, seated astride of his great sea-chest, and sailing through Hell Gate, which just then began to roar and bellow with redoubled fury.

While all the gossip world was thus filled with talk and rumor, poor Wolfert lay sick and sorrowfully in his bed, bruised in body and sorely beaten down in mind. His wife and daughter did all they could to bind up his wounds, both corporal and spiritual. The good old dame never stirred from his bedside, where she sat knitting from morning till night; while his daughter busied herself about him with the fondest care. Nor did they lack assistance from abroad. Whatever may be said of the desertion of friends in distress, they had no complaint of the kind to make. Not an old wife of the neighborhood but abandoned her work to crowd to the mansion of Wolfert Webber, to inquire after his health, and the particulars of his story. Not one came moreover without her little pipkin of pennyroyal, sage, balm, or other herb tea, delighted at an opportunity of signalizing her kindness and her doctorship. What drenchings did not the poor Wolfert undergo, and all in vain! It was a moving sight to behold him wasting away day by day; growing thinner and thinner, and ghastlier and ghastlier, and staring with rueful visage from under an old patchwork counterpane, upon the jury

121

of matrons kindly assembled to sigh and groan and look unhappy around him.

Dirk Waldron was the only being that seemed to shed a ray
of sunshine into this house of mourning. He came in with a
cheery look and manly spirit, and tried to reanimate the expiring heart of the poor money-digger, but it was all in vain.
Wolfert was completely done over. If anything was wanting to
complete his despair, it was a notice served upon him in the
midst of his distress, that the corporation were about to run a
new street through the very centre of his cabbage-garden. He
now saw nothing before him but poverty and ruin; his last
reliance, the garden of his forefathers, was to be laid waste,
and what then was to become of his poor wife and child?

His eyes filled with tears as they followed the dutiful Amy
out of the room one morning. Dirk Waldron was seated beside
him; Wolfert grasped his hand, pointed after his daughter, and
for the first time since his illness, broke the silence he had
maintained.

" I am going! " said he, shaking his head feebly, " and
when I am gone — my poor daughter —— "

" Leave her to me, father! " said Dirk, manfully, — " I'll
take care of her! "

Wolfert looked up in the face of the cheery, strapping
youngster, and saw there was none better able to take care of
a woman.

" Enough," said he, — " she is yours! — and now fetch
me a lawyer — let me make my will and die."

The lawyer was brought — a dapper, bustling, round-headed little man, Roorback (or Rollebuck as it was pronounced) by name. At the sight of him the women broke into loud lamentations, for they looked upon the signing of a will as the signing of a death-warrant. Wolfert made a feeble motion for them to be silent. Poor Amy buried her face and her grief in the bed-curtain. Dame Webber resumed her knitting to hide her distress, which betrayed itself however in a pellucid tear, which trickled silently down, and hung at the end of her peaked nose; while the cat, the only unconcerned member of the family, played with the good dame's ball of worsted, as it rolled about the floor.

Wolfert lay on his back, his night-cap drawn over his forehead; his eyes closed; his whole visage the picture of death. He begged the lawyer to be brief, for he felt his end approaching, and that he had no time to lose. The lawyer nibbed his pen, spread out his paper, and prepared to write.

" I give and bequeath," said Wolfert, faintly, " my small farm —— "

" What — all! " exclaimed the lawyer.

Wolfert half opened his eyes and looked upon the lawyer.

" Yes — all," said he.

" What! all that great patch of land with cabbages and sun-flowers, which the corporation is just going to run a main street through? "

" The same," said Wolfert, with a heavy sigh, and sinking back upon his pillow.

" I wish him joy that inherits it! " said the little lawyer, chuckling, and rubbing his hands involuntarily.

123

" What do you mean? " said Wolfert, again opening his eyes.

" That he'll be one of the richest men in the place! " cried little Rollebuck.

The expiring Wolfert seemed to step back from the threshold of existence: his eyes again lighted up; he raised himself in his bed, shoved back his red worsted night-cap, and stared broadly at the lawyer.

" You don't say so! " exclaimed he.

" Faith, but I do! " rejoined the other. — " Why, when that great field and that huge meadow come to be laid out in streets, and cut up into snug building-lots — why, whoever owns it need not pull off his hat to the patroon! "

" Say you so? " cried Wolfert, half thrusting one leg out of bed, " why, then I think I'll not make my will yet! "

To the surprise of everybody the dying man actually recovered. The vital spark, which had glimmered faintly in the socket, received fresh fuel from the oil of gladness, which the little lawyer poured into his soul. It once more burnt up into a flame.

Give physic to the heart, ye who would revive the body of a spirit-broken man! In a few days Wolfert left his room; in a few days more his table was covered with deeds, plans of streets, and building-lots. Little Rollebuck was constantly with him, his right-hand man and adviser; and instead of making his will, assisted in the more agreeable task of making his fortune. In fact, Wolfert Webber was one of those worthy Dutch burghers of the Manhattoes whose fortunes have been

made, in a manner, in spite of themselves; who have tena-
ciously held on to their hereditary acres, raising turnips and
cabbages about the skirts of the city, hardly able to make both
ends meet, until the corporation has cruelly driven streets
through their abodes, and they have suddenly awakened out
of their lethargy, and, to their astonishment, found themselves
rich men.

Before many months had elapsed, a great bustling street
passed through the very centre of the Webber garden, just
where Wolfert had dreamed of finding a treasure. His golden
dream was accomplished; he did indeed find an unlooked-for
source of wealth; for, when his paternal lands were distributed
into building lots, and rented out to safe tenants, instead of

producing a paltry crop of cabbages, they returned him an abundant crop of rent; insomuch that on quarter-day it was a goodly sight to see his tenants knocking at the door, from morning till night, each with a little round-bellied bag of money, a golden produce of the soil.

The ancient mansion of his forefathers was still kept up; but instead of being a little yellow-fronted Dutch house in a garden, it now stood boldly in the midst of a street, the grand home of the neighborhood; for Wolfert enlarged it with a wing on each side, and a cupola or tea-room on top, where he might climb up and smoke his pipe in hot weather: and in the course of time the whole mansion was overrun by the chubby-faced progeny of Amy Webber and Dirk Waldron.

As Wolfert waxed old, and rich, and corpulent, he also set up a great gingerbread-colored carriage, drawn by a pair of black Flanders mares with tails that swept the ground; and to commemorate the origin of his greatness, he had for his crest a full-blown cabbage painted on the pannels, with the pithy motto *ALLES KOPF,* that is to say, ALL HEAD; meaning thereby that he had risen by sheer head-work.

To fill the measure of his greatness, in the fulness of time the renowned Ramm Rapelye slept with his fathers, and Wolfert Webber succeeded to the leather-bottomed arm-chair, in the inn parlor at Corlaer's Hook; where he long reigned greatly honored and respected, insomuch that he was never known to tell a story without its being believed, nor to utter a joke without its being laughed at.

126

GUESTS FROM GIBBET ISLAND

Guests From Gibbet Island

WHOEVER HAS visited the ancient and renowned village of Communipaw may have noticed an old stone building, of most ruinous and sinister appearance. The doors and window-shutters are ready to drop from their hinges; old clothes are stuffed in the broken panes of glass, while legions of half-starved dogs prowl about the premises, and rush out and bark at every passer-by, for your beggarly house in a village is most apt to swarm with profligate and ill-conditioned dogs. What adds to the sinister appearance of this mansion, is a tall frame in front, not a little resembling a gallows, and which looks as if waiting to accommodate some of the inhabitants with a well-merited airing. It is not a gallows, however, but an ancient sign-post; for this dwelling in the golden days of Communipaw was one of the most orderly and peaceful of village taverns, where public affairs were talked and smoked over. In fact, it was in this very building that Oloffe the Dreamer, and his companions, concerted that great voyage of discovery and colonization, in which they explored Buttermilk Channel, were nearly shipwrecked in the strait of Hell-Gate, and finally landed on the island of Manhattan, and founded the great city of New Amsterdam.

Even after the province had been cruelly wrested from the sway of their High Mightinesses by the combined forces of the British and Yankees, this tavern continued its ancient loyalty. It is true, the head of the Prince of Orange disappeared from the sign, a strange bird being painted over it, with the explanatory legend of " Die Wilde Gans," or, The Wild Goose; but this all the world knew to be a sly riddle of the landlord, the worthy Teunis Van Gieson, a knowing man, in a small way, who laid his finger beside his nose and winked, when any one studied the signification of his sign, and observed that his goose was hatching, but would join the flock whenever they flew over the water; an enigma which was the perpetual recreation and delight of the loyal but fat-headed burghers of Communipaw.

Under the sway of this patriotic, though discreet and quiet publican, the tavern continued to flourish in primeval tranquillity, and was the resort of true-hearted Nederlanders, from all parts of Pavonia; who met here quietly and secretly, to smoke and drink the downfall of Briton and Yankee, and success to Admiral Van Tromp.

The only drawback on the comfort of the establishment, was a nephew of mine host, a sister's son, Yan Yost Vanderscamp by name, and a real scamp by nature. This unlucky whipster showed an early propensity to mischief, which he gratified in a small way by playing tricks upon the frequenters of the Wild Goose; putting gunpowder in their pipes, or squibs in their pockets, and astonished them with an explosion, while they sat nodding round the fireplace in the bar-room; and if perchance a worthy burgher from some distant part of Pavonia lingered until dark over his potation, it was odds but young Vanderscamp would slip a brier under his horse's tail, as he mounted, and send him clattering along the road, in neck-or-nothing style, to the infinite astonishment and discomfiture of the rider.

It may be wondered at that mine host of the Wild Goose did not turn such a graceless varlet out of doors; but Teunis Van Gieson was an easy-tempered man, and having no child of his own, looked upon his nephew with almost parental indulgence. His patience and good nature were doomed to be tried by another inmate of his mansion. This was a cross-grained curmudgeon of a negro, named Pluto, who was a kind of enigma in Communipaw. Where he came from, nobody knew. He was found one morning, after a storm, cast like a sea-monster on the strand, in front of the Wild Goose, and lay there, more dead than alive. The neighbors gathered round, and speculated on this production of the deep; whether it were fish or flesh, or a compound of both, commonly yclept a merman. The kind-hearted Teunis Van Gieson, seeing that he wore the human form, took him into his house, and warmed him into life. By degrees, he showed signs of intelligence, and even uttered sounds very much like language, but which no one in Communipaw could understand. Some thought him a negro just from Guinea, who had either fallen overboard, or escaped from a slave-ship. Nothing, however, could ever draw from him any account of his origin. When questioned on the subject, he merely pointed to Gibbet Island, a small rocky islet, which lies in the open bay, just opposite Communipaw, as if that were his native place, though every body knew it had never been inhabited.

In the process of time, he acquired something of the Dutch language, that is to say, he learnt all its vocabulary of oaths and maledictions, with just words sufficient to string them together. " Donder en blicksem! " (thunder and lightning), was the gentlest of his ejaculations. For years he kept about the Wild Goose, more like one of those familiar spirits, or household goblins, we read of, than like a human being. He acknowledged allegiance to no one, but performed various domestic offices, when it suited his humor; waiting occasionally on the guests; grooming the horses, cutting wood, drawing water; and all this without being ordered. Lay any command on him, and the stubborn sea-urchin was sure to rebel. He was never so much at home, however, as when on the water, plying about in skiff or canoe, entirely alone, fishing, crabbing, or grabbing for oysters, and would bring home quantities for the larder of the Wild Goose, which he would throw down at the kitchen door, with a growl. No wind nor weather deterred him from launching forth on his favorite element: indeed, the wilder the weather, the more he seemed to enjoy it. If a storm was brewing, he was sure to put off from shore; and would be seen far out in the bay, his light skiff dancing like a feather on the waves, when sea and sky were in a turmoil, and the stoutest ships were fain to lower their sails. Sometimes on such occasions he would be absent for days together. How he weathered the tempest, and how and where he subsisted, no one could divine, nor did any one venture to for all had an almost superstitious awe of him. Some of the Communipaw oystermen declared they had more than once seen him suddenly disappear, canoe and all, as if plunged beneath the waves, and after a while come up again, in quite a different part of the bay; whence they concluded that he could live under water like that notable species of wild duck,

133

commonly called the hell-diver. All began to consider him in
the light of a foul-weather bird, like the Mother Carey's
Chicken, or stormy petrel; and whenever they saw him putting far out in his skiff, in cloudy weather, made up their minds
for a storm.

The only being for whom he seemed to have any liking,
was Yan Yost Vanderscamp, and him he liked for his very
wickedness. He in a manner took the boy under his tutelage,
prompted him to all kinds of mischief, aided him in every wild
harum-scarum freak, until the lad became the complete scapegrace of the village; a pest to his uncle, and to every one else.
Nor were his pranks confined to the land; he soon learned to
accompany old Pluto on the water. Together these worthies
would cruise about the broad bay, and all the neighboring
straits and rivers; poking around in skiffs and canoes; robbing
the set nets of the fishermen; landing on remote coasts, and

laying waste orchards and watermelon patches; in short, carrying on a complete system of piracy, on a small scale. Piloted by Pluto, the youthful Vanderscamp soon became acquainted with all the bays, rivers, creeks, and inlets of the watery world around him; could navigate from the Hook to Spiting-devil on the darkest night, and learned to set even the terrors of Hell Gate at defiance.

At length, negro and boy suddenly disappeared, and days and weeks elapsed, but without tidings of them. Some said they must have run away and gone to sea; others jocosely hinted, that old Pluto, being no other than his namesake in disguise, had spirited away the boy to the nether regions. All, however, agreed in one thing, that the village was well rid of them.

In the process of time, the good Teunis Van Gieson slept with his fathers, and the tavern remained shut up, waiting for a claimant, for the next heir was Yan Yost Vanderscamp, and he had not been heard of for years. At length, one day, a boat was seen pulling for shore, from a long, black, rakish-looking schooner, that lay at anchor in the bay. The boat's crew seemed worthy of the craft from which they debarked. Never had such a set of noisy, roistering, swaggering varlets landed in peaceful Communipaw. They were outlandish in garb and demeanor, and were headed by a rough, burly, bully ruffian, with fiery whiskers, a copper nose, a scar across his face, and a great Flaunderish beaver slouched on one side of his head, in whom, to their dismay, the quiet inhabitants were made to recognise their early pest, Yan Yost Vanderscamp. The rear of this hopeful gang was brought up by old Pluto, who had lost an eye, grown grizzly-headed, and looked more like a devil than ever. Vanderscamp renewed his acquaintance with the old burghers, much against their will, and in a manner not at all to their taste. He slapped them familiarly on the back, gave them an iron grip of the hand, and was hail fellow well met. According to his own account, he had been all the world over, had made money by bags full, had ships in every sea, and now meant to turn the Wild Goose into a country-seat, where he and his comrades, all rich merchants from foreign parts, might enjoy themselves in the interval of their voyages.

Sure enough, in a little while there was a complete metamorphose of the Wild Goose. From being a quiet, peaceful Dutch public-house, it became a most riotous, uproarious private dwelling; a complete rendezvous for boisterous men of the seas, who came here to have what they called a " blow out " on dry land, and might be seen at all hours, lounging about the door, or lolling out of the windows; swearing among themselves, and cracking rough jokes on every passer-by. The house was fitted up too, in so strange a manner: hammocks slung to the walls, instead of bedsteads; odd kinds of furniture, of foreign fashion; bamboo couches, Spanish chairs; pistols, cutlasses, and blunderbusses, suspended on every peg; silver crucifixes on the mantelpieces, silver candlesticks and porringers on the tables, contrasting oddly with the pewter and Delf ware of the original establishment. And then the strange amusements of these sea-monsters! Pitching Spanish dollars, instead of quoits; firing blunderbusses out of the window;

The UNWELCOME RETURN

shooting at a mark, or at any unhappy dog, or cat, or barn-door fowl, that might happen to come within reach.

The only being who seemed to relish their rough waggery, was old Pluto; and yet he led but a dog's life of it; for they practised all kinds of manual jokes upon him; kicked him about like a football; shook him by his grizzly mop of wool, and never spoke to him without coupling a curse by way of adjective to his name, and consigning him to the infernal regions. The old fellow, however, seemed to like them the better, the more they cursed him, though his utmost expression of pleasure never amounted to more than the growl of a petted bear, when his ears are rubbed.

Old Pluto was the ministering spirit at the orgies of the Wild Goose; and such orgies as took place there! Such drinking, singing, whooping, swearing; with an occasional interlude of quarrelling and fighting. The noisier grew the revel, the more old Pluto plied the potations, until the guests would become frantic in their merriment, smashing everything to pieces, and throwing the house out of the windows. Sometimes, after a drinking bout, they sallied forth and scoured the village, to the dismay of the worthy burghers, who gathered their women within doors, and would have shut up the house. Vanderscamp, however, was not to be rebuffed. He insisted on renewing acquaintance with his old neighbors, and on introducing his friends, the merchants, to their families; swore he was on the look-out for a wife, and meant, before he stopped, to find husbands for all their daughters. So, will-ye, nill-ye, sociable he was; swaggered about their best parlors, with his hat on one

side of his head; sat on the good wife's nicely-waxed mahogany table, kicking his heels against the carved and polished legs; kissed and tousled the young vrouws; and, if they frowned and pouted, gave them a gold rosary, or sparkling cross, to put them in good humor again.

Sometimes nothing would satisfy him, but he must have some of his old neighbors to dinner at the Wild Goose. There was no refusing him, for he had the complete upper hand of the community, and the peaceful burghers all stood in awe of him. But what a time would the quiet, worthy men have, among these rake-hells, who would delight to astound them with the most extravagant gunpowder tales, embroidered with all kinds of foreign oaths, clink the can with them, pledge them in deep potations, bawl drinking songs in their ears, and occasionally fire pistols over their heads, or under the table, and then laugh in their faces, and ask them how they liked the smell of gunpowder.

Thus was the little village of Communipaw for a time like the unfortunate wight possessed with devils; until Vanderscamp and his brother merchants would sail on another trading voyage, when the Wild Goose would be shut up, and every thing relapse into quiet, only to be disturbed by his next visitation.

The mystery of all these proceedings gradually dawned upon the tardy intellects of Communipaw. These were the times of the notorious Captain Kidd, when the American harbors were the resorts of piratical adventurers of all kinds, who, under pretext of mercantile voyages, scoured the West Indies, made plundering descents upon the Spanish Main, visited even the remote Indian Seas, and then came to dispose of their booty, have their revels, and fit out new expeditions, in the English colonies.

Vanderscamp had served in this hopeful school, and having risen to importance among the buccaneers, had pitched upon his native village and early home, as a quiet, out-of-the-way, unsuspected place, where he and his comrades, while anchored at New York, might have their feasts, and concert their plans, without molestation.

At length the attention of the British government was called to these piratical enterprises, that were becoming so frequent and outrageous. Vigorous measures were taken to check and punish them. Several of the most noted freebooters were caught and executed, and three of Vanderscamp's chosen comrades, the most riotous swashbucklers of the Wild Goose, were hanged in chains on Gibbet Island, in full sight of their favorite resort. As to Vanderscamp himself, he and his man Pluto again disappeared, and it was hoped by the people of Communipaw that he had fallen in some foreign brawl, or been swung on some foreign gallows.

For a time, therefore, the tranquillity of the village was restored; the worthy Dutchmen once more smoked their pipes in peace, eyeing, with peculiar complacency their old pests and terrors, the pirates, dangling and drying in the sun, on Gibbet Island.

This perfect calm was doomed at length to be ruffled. The fiery persecution of the pirates gradually subsided. Justice was satisfied with the examples that had been made, and there was no more talk of Kidd, and the other heroes of like kidney. On a calm summer evening, a boat, somewhat heavily laden, was seen pulling into Communipaw. What was the surprise and disquiet of the inhabitants, to see Yan Yost Vanderscamp seated at the helm, and his man Pluto tugging at the oar! Vanderscamp, however, was apparently an altered man. He brought home with him a wife, who seemed to be a shrew, and to have the upper hand of him. He no longer was the swaggering, bully ruffian, but affected the regular merchant, and talked of retiring from business, and settling down quietly, to pass the rest of his days in his native place.

The Wild Goose mansion was again opened, but with diminished splendor, and no riot. It is true, Vanderscamp had frequent nautical visitors, and the sound of revelry was occasionally overheard in his house; but everything seemed to be done under the rose, and old Pluto was the only servant that officiated at these orgies. The visitors, indeed, were by no means

142

of the turbulent stamp of their predecessors; but quiet, mysterious traders, full of nods, and winks, and hieroglyphic signs, with whom, to use their cant phrase, " everything was smug." Their ships came to anchor at night, in the lower bay; and on a private signal, Vanderscamp would launch his boat, and accompanied solely by his man Pluto, would make them mysterious visits. Sometimes boats pulled in at night, in front of the Wild Goose, and various articles of merchandise were landed in the dark, and spirited away, nobody knew whither. One of the more curious of the inhabitants kept watch, and caught a glimpse of the features of some of these night visitors, by the casual glance of a lantern, and declared that he recognized more than one of the freebooting frequenters of the Wild Goose, in former times; whence he concluded that Vanderscamp was at his old game, and that this mysterious merchandise was nothing more nor less than piratical plunder. The more charitable opinion, however, was that Vanderscamp and his comrades, having been driven from their old line of business, by the " oppressions of government," had resorted to smuggling to make both ends meet.

Be that as it may: I come now to the extraordinary fact, which is the butt-end of this story. It happened late one night, that Yan Yost Vanderscamp was returning across the broad bay, in his light skiff, rowed by his man Pluto. He had been carousing on board of a vessel, newly arrived, and was somewhat obfuscated in intellect by the liquor he had imbibed. It was a still, sultry night; a heavy mass of lurid clouds was rising in the west, with the low muttering of distant thunder.

Vanderscamp called on Pluto to pull lustily, that they might get home before the gathering storm. The old negro made no reply, but shaped his course so as to skirt the rocky shores of Gibbet Island. A faint creaking overhead caused Vanderscamp to cast up his eyes, when to his horror, he beheld the bodies of his three pot companions and brothers in iniquity dangling in the moonlight, their rags fluttering, and their chains creaking, as they were slowly swung backward and forward by the rising breeze.

"What do you mean, you blockhead!" cried Vanderscamp, "by pulling so close to the island?"

"I thought you'd be glad to see your old friends once more," growled the negro: "you were never afraid of a living man, what do you fear from the dead?"

"Who's afraid?" hicupped Vanderscamp, partly heated by liquor, partly nettled by the jeer of the negro; "who's afraid! Hang me, but I would be glad to see them once more, alive or dead, at the Wild Goose. Come, my lads in the wind!" continued he, taking a draught, and flourishing the bottle above his head, "here's fair weather to you in the other world; and if you should be walking the rounds to-night, odds fish! but I'll be happy if you will drop in to supper."

A dismal creaking was the only reply. The wind blew loud and shrill, and as it whistled round the gallows, and among the bones, sounded as if they were laughing and gibbering in the air. Old Pluto chuckled to himself, and now pulled for home. The storm burst over the voyagers, while they were yet far from shore. The rain fell in torrents, the

144

thunder crashed and pealed, and the lightning kept up an incessant blaze. It was stark midnight before they landed at Communipaw.

Dripping and shivering, Vanderscamp crawled homeward. He was completely sobered by the storm; the water soaked from without, having diluted and cooled the liquor within. Arrived at the Wild Goose, he knocked timidly and dubiously at the door, for he dreaded the reception he was to experience from his wife. He had reason to do so. She met him at the threshold, in a precious ill-humor.

" Is this a time," said she, " to keep people out of their beds, and to bring home company, to turn the house upside down? "

" Company? " said Vanderscamp, meekly; " I have brought no company with me, wife."

" No indeed! they have got here before you, but by your invitation; and blessed-looking company they are, truly! "

Vanderscamp's knees smote together. " For the love of heaven, where are they, wife? "

"Where? — why in the blue room up stairs, making themselves as much at home as if the house were their own."

Vanderscamp made a desperate effort, scrambled up to the room, and threw open the door. Sure enough, there at a table, on which burned a light as blue as brimstone, sat the three guests from Gibbet Island, with halters round their necks, and bobbing their cups together, as if they were hob-or-nobbing, and trolling the old Dutch freebooter's glee, since translated into English:

> "*For three merry lads be we,*
> *And three merry lads be we;*
> *I on the land, and thou on the sand,*
> *And Jack on the gallows-tree.*"

Vanderscamp saw and heard no more. Starting back with horror, he missed his footing on the landing-place, and fell from the top of the stairs to the bottom. He was taken up speechless, and, either from the fall or the fright, was buried in the yard of the little Dutch church at Bergen, on the following Sunday.

From that day forward, the fate of the Wild Goose was sealed. It was pronounced a *haunted house*, and avoided accordingly. No one inhabited it but Vanderscamp's shrew of a widow, and old Pluto, and they were considered but little better than its hobgoblin visitors. Pluto grew more and more haggard and morose, and looked more like an imp of darkness than a human being. He spoke to no one, but went about muttering to himself; or, as some hinted, talking with the devil, who, though unseen, was ever at his elbow. Now and then he was seen pulling about the bay alone in his skiff, in dark weather, or at the approach of nightfall; nobody could tell why, unless on an errand to invite more guests from the gallows. Indeed it was affirmed that the Wild Goose still continued to be a house of entertainment for such guests, and that on stormy nights, the blue chamber was occasionally illuminated, and sounds of diabolical merriment were overheard, mingling with the howling of the tempest. Some treated these as idle stories, until on one such night, it was about the time of the equinox, there was a horrible uproar in the Wild Goose, that could not be mistaken. It was not so much the sound of revelry, however, as strife, with two or three piercing shrieks, that pervaded every part of the village. Nevertheless, no one thought of hastening to the spot. On the contrary, the honest burghers of Communipaw drew their nightcaps over their ears, and buried their heads under the bedclothes, at the thoughts of Vanderscamp and his gallows companions.

The next morning, some of the bolder and more curious undertook to reconnoitre. All was quiet and lifeless at the Wild Goose. The door yawned wide open, and had evidently been open all night, for the storm had beaten into the house. Gathering more courage from the silence and apparent desertion, they gradually ventured over the threshold. The house had indeed the air of having been possessed by devils. Every thing was topsy-turvy; trunks had been broken open, and chests

148

of drawers and corner cupboards turned inside out, as in a time of general sack and pillage; but the most woeful sight was the widow of Yan Yost Vanderscamp, extended a corpse on the floor of the blue chamber, with the marks of a deadly gripe on the windpipe.

All now was conjecture and dismay at Communipaw; and the disappearance of old Pluto, who was nowhere to be found, gave rise to all kinds of wild surmises. Some suggested that the negro had betrayed the house to some of Vanderscamp's buccaneering associates, and that they had decamped together with the booty; others surmised that the negro was nothing more nor less than a devil incarnate, who had now accomplished his ends, and made off with his dues.

Events, however, vindicated the negro from this last imputation. His skiff was picked up, drifting about the bay, bottom upward, as if wrecked in a tempest; and his body was found, shortly afterward, by some Communipaw fishermen, stranded among the rocks of Gibbet Island, near the foot of the pirates' gallows. The fishermen shook their heads, and observed that old Pluto had ventured once too often to invite Guests from Gibbet Island.

DOLPH HEYLIGER

DOLPH HEYLIGER

Dolph Heyliger

IN THE early time of the province of New York, while it groaned under the tyranny of the English governor, Lord Cornbury, who carried his cruelties towards the Dutch inhabitants so far as to allow no dominie or schoolmaster to officiate in their language without his special license, there lived in the jolly little old city of the Manhattoes a kind, motherly dame, known by the name of Dame Heyliger. She was the widow of a Dutch sea-captain, who died suddenly of a fever, in consequence of working too hard and eating too heartily, at a time when all the inhabitants turned out in a panic, to fortify the place against the invasion of a small French privateer.[1] He left her with very little money and one infant son, the only survivor of several children. The good woman had need of much management to make both ends meet, and keep up a decent appearance. However, as her husband had fallen a victim to his zeal for the public safety, it was universally agreed that " something ought to be done for the widow "; and on the hopes of this " something " she lived tolerably for some years; in the meantime everybody pitied and spoke well of her, and that helped along.

She lived in a small house, in a small street, called Garden Street, very probably from a garden which may have flourished

[1] 1705

153

there some time or other. As her necessities every year grew greater, and the talk of the public about doing " something for her " grew less, she had to cast about for some mode of doing something for herself, by way of helping out her slender means, and maintaining her independence, of which she was somewhat tenacious.

Living in a mercantile town, she had caught something of the spirit, and determined to venture a little in the great lottery of commerce. On a sudden, therefore, to the great surprise of the street, there appeared at her window a grand array of gingerbread kings and queens, with their arms stuck akimbo, after the invariable royal manner. There were also several broken tumblers, some filled with sugar-plums, some with marbles; there were, moreover, cakes of various kinds, and barley-sugar, and Holland dolls, and wooden horses, with here and there gilt-covered picture-books, and now and then a skein of thread, or a dangling pound of candles. At the door of the house sat the good old dame's cat, a decent demure-looking personage, who seemed to scan everybody that passed, to criticise their dress, and now and then to stretch her neck, and to look out with sudden curiosity to see what was going on at the other end of the street; but if by chance any idle vagabond dog came by, and offered to be uncivil — hoity-toity! — how she would bristle up, and growl, and spit, and strike out her paws!

But though the good woman had to come down to those humble means of subsistence, yet she still kept up a feeling of family pride, being descended from the Vanderspiegels of

Amsterdam; and she had the family arms painted and framed, and hung over her mantel-piece. Her house was quite a resort of the old wives of the neighborhood; they would drop in there of a winter's afternoon, as she sat knitting on one side of her fireplace, her cat purring on the other, and the tea-kettle singing before it; and they would gossip with her until late in the evening. There was always an arm-chair for Peter de Groodt, sometimes called Long Peter, and sometimes Peter Longlegs, the clerk and sexton of the little Lutheran church, who was her great crony, and indeed the oracle of her fireside. Nay, the Dominie himself did not disdain, now and then, to step in, converse about the state of her mind, and take a glass of her special good cherry-brandy. Indeed, he never failed to call on New-Year's day, and wish her a happy New Year; and the good dame, who was a little vain on some points, always piqued herself on giving him as large a cake as any one in town.

I have said that she had one son. He was the child of her old age; but could hardly be called the comfort, for, of all unlucky urchins, Dolph Heyliger was the most mischievous. Not that the whipster was really vicious; he was only full of fun and frolic, and had that daring, gamesome spirit which is extolled in a rich man's child, but execrated in a poor man's. He was continually getting into scrapes; his mother was incessantly harassed with complaints of some waggish pranks which he had played off; bills were sent in for windows that he had broken; he had not reached his fourteenth year before he was pronounced, by all the neighborhood, to be a " wicked dog, the wickedest dog in the street! " Nay, one old gentleman, in a

156

claret-colored coat, with a thin red face, and ferret eyes, went so far as to assure Dame Heyliger, that her son would, one day or other, come to the gallows!

Yet, notwithstanding all this, the poor old soul loved her boy. It seemed as though she loved him the better the worse he behaved, and that he grew more in her favor the more he grew out of favor with the world. Mothers are foolish, fond-hearted beings; there's no reasoning them out of their dotage; and, indeed, this poor woman's child was all that was left to love her in this world; so we must not think it hard that she turned a deaf ear to her good friends, who sought to prove to her that Dolph would come to a halter.

To do the varlet justice, too, he was strongly attached to his parent. He would not willingly have given her pain on any account; and when he had been doing wrong, it was but for him to catch his poor mother's eye fixed wistfully and sorrowfully upon him to fill his heart with bitterness and contrition. But he was a heedless youngster and could not, for the life of him, resist any new temptation to fun and mischief. Though quick at his learning, whenever he could be brought to apply himself, he was always prone to be led away by idle company, and would play truant to hunt after birds' nests, to rob orchards, or to swim in the Hudson.

In this way he grew up, a tall, lubberly boy; and his mother began to be greatly perplexed what to do with him, or how to put him in a way to do for himself; for he had acquired such an unlucky reputation, that no one seemed willing to employ him.

Many were the consultations that she held with Peter de Groodt, the clerk and sexton, who was her prime counsellor. Peter was as much perplexed as herself, for he had no great opinion of the boy, and thought he would never come to good. He at once advised her to send him to sea; a piece of advice only given in the most desperate cases; but Dame Heyliger would not listen to such an idea; she could not think of letting Dolph go out of her sight. She was sitting one day knitting by her fireside, in great perplexity, when the sexton entered with an air of unusual vivacity and briskness. He had just come from a funeral. It had been that of a boy of Dolph's years, who had been apprentice to a famous German doctor, and had died of a consumption.

Peter de Groodt entered the house of Dame Heyliger with unusual alacrity. A bright idea had popped into his head at the funeral, over which he had chuckled as he shovelled the earth into the grave of the doctor's disciple. It had occurred to him, that, as the situation of the deceased was vacant at the doctor's, it would be the very place for Dolph. The boy had parts, and could pound a pestle, and run an errand with any boy in the town; and what more was wanted in a student?

The suggestion of the sage Peter was a vision of glory to the mother. She already saw Dolph, in her mind's eye, with a cane at his nose, a knocker at his door, and an M.D. at the end of his name, — one of the established dignitaries of the town.

The matter, once undertaken, was soon effected; the sexton had some influence with the doctor, they having had much dealing together in the way of their separate professions; and the very next morning he called and conducted the urchin, clad in his Sunday clothes, to undergo the inspection of Dr. Karl Lodovick Knipperhausen.

They found the doctor seated in an elbow-chair, in one corner of his study, or laboratory, with a large volume, in German print, before him. He was a short fat man, with a dark square face, rendered more dark by a black velvet cap. He had a little nobbed nose, not unlike the ace of spades, with a pair of spectacles gleaming on each side of his dusky countenance, like a couple of bow-windows.

Dolph felt struck with awe on entering into the presence of this learned man; and gazed about him with boyish wonder at the furniture of this chamber of knowledge; which appeared to him almost as the den of a magician. In the centre stood a claw-footed table, with pestle and mortar, phials and gallipots, and a pair of small burnished scales. At one end was a heavy clothes-press, turned into a receptacle for drugs and compounds; against which hung the doctor's hat and cloak, and gold-headed cane, and on the top grinned a human skull. Along the mantelpiece were glass vessels, in which were snakes and lizards, and a human fœtus preserved in spirits. A closet, the doors of which were taken off, contained three whole shelves of books, and some, too, of mighty folio dimensions, — a collection the like of which Dolph had never before beheld. As the library did not take up the whole of the closet, the doctor's thrifty housekeeper had occupied the rest with pots of pickles and preserves; and had hung about the room, among awful

159

implements of the healing art, strings of red pepper and corpulent cucumbers, carefully preserved for seed.

Peter de Groodt and his protégé were received with great gravity and stateliness by the doctor, who was a very wise, dignified little man, and never smiled. He surveyed Dolph from head to foot, above, and under, and through his spectacles, and the poor lad's heart quailed as these great glasses glared on him like two full moons. The doctor heard all that Peter de Groodt had to say in favor of the youthful candidate; and then wetting his thumb with the end of his tongue, he began deliberately to turn over page after page of the great black volume before him. At length, after many hums and haws, and strokings of the chin, and all that hesitation and deliberation with which a wise man proceeds to do what he intended to do from the very first, the doctor agreed to take the lad as a disciple; to give him bed, board, and clothing, and to instruct him in the healing art; in return for which he was to have his services until his twenty-first year.

Behold, then, our hero, all at once transformed from an unlucky urchin running wild about the streets, to a student of medicine, diligently pounding a pestle, under the auspices of the learned Doctor Karl Lodovick Knipperhausen. It was a happy transition for his fond old mother. She was delighted with the idea of her boy's being brought up worthy of his ancestors; and anticipated the day when he would be able to hold up his head with the lawyer, that lived in the large house opposite; or, peradventure, with the Dominie himself.

Doctor Knipperhausen was a native of the Palatinate in

DOCTOR KARL LODOVICK KNIPPERHAUSEN

Germany; whence, in company with many of his countrymen, he had taken refuge in England, on account of religious persecution. He was one of nearly three thousand Palatines, who came over from England in 1710, under the protection of Governor Hunter. Where the doctor had studied, how he had acquired his medical knowledge, and where he had received his diploma, it is hard at present to say, for nobody knew at the time; yet it is certain that his profound skill and abstruse knowledge were the talk and wonder of the common people, far and near.

Some of his admirers even went so far as to say, that he knew more than the governor himself.

No sooner was Dolph received into the doctor's family, than he was put in possession of the lodging of his predecessor. It was a garret room of a steep-roofed Dutch house, where the rain had pattered on the shingles, and the lightning gleamed, and the wind piped through the crannies in stormy weather; and where whole troops of hungry rats, like Don Cossacks, galloped about, in defiance of traps and ratsbane.

He was soon up to his ears in medical studies, being employed, morning, noon and night, in rolling pills, filtering tinctures, or pounding the pestle and mortar in one corner of the laboratory; while the doctor would take his seat in another corner, when he had nothing else to do, or expected visitors, and arrayed in his morning-gown and velvet cap, would pore over the contents of some folio volume. It is true, that the regular thumping of Dolph's pestle, or perhaps the drowsy buzzing of the summer flies, would now and then lull the little man into a slumber; but then his spectacles were always wide awake, and studiously regarding the book.

There was another personage in the house, however, to whom Dolph was obliged to pay allegiance. Though a bachelor, and a man of such great dignity and importance, the doctor was, like many other wise men, subject to petticoat government. He was completely under the sway of his housekeeper, — a spare, busy, fretting housewife, in a little, round, quilted German cap, with a huge bunch of keys jingling at the girdle of an exceedingly long waist. Frau Ilsé had accompanied him in his various migrations from Germany to England, and from England to the province; managing his establishment and himself too; ruling him, it is true, with a gentle hand, but carrying a high hand with all the world beside.

She was one of those prying gossips who know every one's business better than they do themselves; and whose all-seeing eyes, and all-telling tongues, are terrors throughout a neighborhood.

Nothing of any moment transpired in the world of scandal of this little burgh, but it was known to Frau Ilsy. She had her crew of cronies, that were perpetually hurrying to her little parlor with some precious bit of news, nay, she would sometimes discuss a whole volume of secret history, as she held the street-door ajar, and gossiped with one of these garrulous cronies in the very teeth of a December blast.

Between the doctor and the housekeeper it may easily be supposed that Dolph had a busy life of it. As Frau Ilsy kept the keys, and literally ruled the roost, it was starvation to offend

163

1697

GOSSIP.

her, though he found the study of her temper more perplexing even than that of medicine. When not busy in the laboratory, she kept him running hither and thither on her errands; and on Sundays he was obliged to accompany her to and from church, and carry her Bible. Many a time has the poor varlet stood shivering and blowing his fingers, or holding his frost-bitten nose, in the churchyard, while Ilsy and her cronies were huddled together, wagging their heads, and tearing some unlucky character to pieces.

With all his advantages, however, Dolph made very slow progress in his art. This was no fault of the doctor's, certainly, for he took unwearied pains with the lad, keeping him close to the pestle and mortar, or on the trot about town with phials and pill-boxes; and if he ever flagged in his industry, which he was rather apt to do, the doctor would fly into a passion, and ask him if he ever expected to learn his profession, unless he applied himself closer to the study. The fact is, he still retained the fondness for sport and mischief that had marked his child-hood; the habit, indeed, had strengthened with his years, and gained force from being thwarted and constrained. He daily grew more and more untractable, and lost favor in the eyes, both of the doctor and the housekeeper.

In the meantime the doctor went on, waxing wealthy and renowned. He was famous for his skill in managing cases not laid down in the books. He had cured several old women and young girls of witchcraft. He had even restored one strapping country girl to perfect health, who had gone so far as to vomit crooked pins and needles; which is considered a desperate stage of the malady. It was whispered, also, that he was possessed of the art of preparing love-powders; and many applications had he in consequence from lovesick patients of both sexes. But all these cases formed the mysterious part of his practice, in which, according to the cant phrase, " secrecy and honor might be depended on." Dolph, therefore, was obliged to turn out of the study whenever such consultations occurred, though it is said he learnt more of the secrets of the art at the keyhole than by all the rest of his studies put together.

As the doctor increased in wealth, he began to extend his possessions, and to look forward, like other great men, to the time when he should retire to the repose of a country-seat. For this purpose he had purchased a farm, or as the Dutch settlers called it, a *bowerie,* a few miles from town. It had been the residence of a wealthy family, that had returned some time since to Holland. A large mansion-house stood in the centre of it, very much out of repair, and which, in consequence of certain reports, had received the appellation of the Haunted House. Either from these reports, or from its actual dreariness, the doctor found it impossible to get a tenant; and that the place might not fall to ruin before he could reside in it himself, he placed a country boor, with his family, in one wing, with the privilege of cultivating the farm on shares.

The doctor now felt all the dignity of a landholder rising within him. He began to complain of the fatigue of business; and was fond of riding out " to look at his estate." His little expeditions to his lands were attended with a bustle and parade that created a sensation throughout the neighborhood. His wall-eyed horse stood, stamping and whisking off the flies, for a full hour before the house. Then the doctor's saddle-bags would be brought out and adjusted; then, after a little while, his cloak would be rolled up and strapped to the saddle; then his umbrella would be buttoned to the cloak; while, in the meantime, a group of ragged boys would gather before the door. At length the doctor would issue forth, in a pair of jack-boots that reached above his knees, and a cocked hat flapped down in front. As he was a short, fat man, he took some time to mount into the saddle; and when there, he took some time to have the saddle and stirrups properly adjusted, enjoying the wonder and admiration of the urchin crowd. Even after he had set off, he would pause in the middle of the street, or trot back two or three times to give some parting orders; which were answered by the housekeeper from the door, or Dolph from the study, or the black cook from the cellar, or the chambermaid from the garret window; and there were generally some last words bawled after him, just as he was turning the corner.

The whole neighborhood would be aroused by this pomp and circumstance. The cobbler would leave his last; the barber would thrust out his frizzled head, with a comb sticking in it; a knot would collect at the grocer's door, and the word would be buzzed from one end of the street to the other, " The doctor's riding out to his country-seat! "

These were golden moments for Dolph. No sooner was the doctor out of sight, than pestle and mortar were abandoned; the laboratory was left to take care of itself, and the student was off on some mad-cap frolic.

He was the ringleader of all holiday sports and midnight gambols; ready for all kinds of mischievous pranks and hare-brained adventures.

There is nothing so troublesome as a hero on a small scale, or, rather, a hero in a small town. Dolph soon became the abhorrence of all drowsy, housekeeping old citizens, who hated noise, and had no relish for waggery. The good dames, too, considered him as little better than a reprobate, gathered their daughters under their wings whenever he approached, and pointed him out as a warning to their sons. No one seemed to hold him in much regard except the wild striplings of the place, who were captivated by his open-hearted, daring manners, — and the negroes, who always looked upon every idle, do-nothing youngster as a kind of gentleman. Even the good Peter de Groodt, who had considered himself a kind of patron of the lad, began to despair of him; and would shake his head

168

dubiously, as he listened to a long complaint from the house-keeper, and sipped a glass of her raspberry brandy.

Still his mother was not to be wearied out of her affection by all the waywardness of her boy; nor disheartened by the stories of his misdeeds, with which her good friends were continually regaling her. She had, it is true, very little of the pleasure which rich people enjoy, in always hearing their children praised; but she considered all this ill-will as a kind of persecution which he suffered, and she liked him the better on that account. She saw him growing up a fine, tall, good-looking youngster, and she looked at him with the secret pride of a mother's heart. It was her great desire that Dolph should appear like a gentleman, and all the money she could save went towards helping out his pocket and his wardrobe. She would look out of the window after him, as he sallied forth in his best array, and her heart would yearn with delight; and once, when Peter de Groodt, struck with the youngster's gallant appearance on a bright Sunday morning, observed, " Well, after all, Dolph does grow a comely fellow! " the tear of pride started into the mother's eye. " Ah, neighbor! neighbor! " exclaimed she, " they may say what they please; poor Dolph will yet hold up his head with the best of them! "

Dolph Heyliger had now nearly attained his one-and-twentieth year, and the term of his medical studies was just expiring; yet it must be confessed that he knew little more of the profession than when he first entered the doctor's doors. This, however, could not be from any want of quickness of parts, for he showed amazing aptness in mastering other

169

branches of knowledge, which he could only have studied at intervals. He was, for instance, a sure marksman, and won all the geese and turkeys at Christmas holidays. He was a bold rider; he was famous for leaping and wrestling; he played tolerably on the fiddle; could swim like a fish; and was the best hand in the whole place at fives and ninepins.

All these accomplishments, however, procured him no favor in the eyes of the doctor, who grew more and more crabbed and intolerant the nearer the term of apprenticeship approached. Frau Ilsy, too, was forever finding some occasion to raise a windy tempest about his ears, and seldom encountered him about the house without a clatter of the tongue; so that at length the jingling of her keys, as she approached, was to Dolph like the ringing of the prompter's bell, that gives notice of a theatrical thunder-storm. Nothing but the infinite good-humor of the heedless youngster enabled him to bear all this domestic tyranny without open rebellion. It was evident that the doctor and his housekeeper were preparing to beat the poor youth out of the nest, the moment his term should have expired — a short-hand mode which the doctor had of providing for useless disciples.

Indeed, the little man had been rendered more than usually irritable lately in consequence of various cares and vexations which his country estate had brought upon him. The doctor had been repeatedly annoyed by the rumors and tales which prevailed concerning the old mansion, and found it difficult to prevail even upon the country-man and his family to remain there rent-free. Every time he rode out to the farm he was teased by some fresh complaint of strange noises and fearful sights, with which the tenants were disturbed at night; and the doctor would come home fretting and fuming, and vent his spleen upon the whole household. He was threatened with an absolute loss of the profits of his property; and then, what a blow to his territorial consequence, to be the landlord of a haunted house!

It was observed, however, that with all his vexation, the doctor never proposed to sleep in the house himself; nay, he could never be prevailed upon to remain on the premises after dark, but made the best of his way for town as soon as the bats began to flit about in the twilight. The fact was, the doctor had a secret belief in ghosts, having passed the early part of his life in a country where they particularly abound; and indeed the story went, that, when a boy, he had once seen the devil upon the Hartz Mountains in Germany.

At length the doctor's vexations on this head were brought to a crisis. One morning as he sat dozing over a volume in his study, he was suddenly startled from his slumbers by the bustling in of the housekeeper.

" Here's a fine to do! " cried she, as she entered the room. " Here's Claus Hopper come in, bag and baggage, from the farm, and swears he'll have nothing more to do with it. The whole family have been frightened out of their wits; for there's such racketing and rummaging about the old house, that they can't sleep quiet in their beds! "

" Donner and blitzen! " cried the doctor, impatiently; " will they never have done chattering about that house? What a pack of fools, to let a few rats and mice frighten them out of good quarters! "

" Nay, nay," said the housekeeper, wagging her head knowingly, and piqued at having a good ghost-story doubted, " there's more in it than rats and mice. All the neighborhood talks about the house; and then such sights as have been seen in it! Peter de Groodt tells me that the family that sold you the house, and went to Holland, dropped several strange hints about it, and said, ' they wished you joy of your bargain '; and you know yourself there's no getting any family to live in it."

" Peter de Groodt's a ninny — an old woman," said the doctor, peevishly; " I'll warrant he's been filling these people's heads full of stories. It's just like his nonsense about the ghost that haunted the church belfry, as an excuse for not ringing the bell that cold night when Harmanus Brinkerhoff's house was on fire. Send Claus to me."

Claus Hopper now made his appearance: a simple country lout, full of awe at finding himself in the very study of Dr.

Knipperhausen, and too much embarrassed to enter in much detail of the matters that had caused his alarm. He stood twirling his hat in one hand, resting sometimes on one leg, sometimes on the other, looking occasionally at the doctor, and now and then stealing a fearful glance at the death's-head that seemed ogling him from the top of the clothes-press.

The doctor tried every means to persuade him to return to the farm, but all in vain; he maintained a dogged determination on the subject; and at the close of every argument or solicitation would make the same brief, inflexible reply: " Ich kan nicht, mynheer." The doctor was a " little pot, and soon hot "; his patience was exhausted by these continual vexations about his estate. The stubborn refusal of Claus Hopper seemed to him like flat rebellion; his temper suddenly boiled over, and Claus was glad to make a rapid retreat to escape scalding.

When the bumpkin got to the housekeeper's room, he found Peter de Groodt, and several other true believers, ready to receive him. Here he indemnified himself for the restraint he had suffered in the study, and opened a budget of stories about the haunted house that astonished all his hearers. The housekeeper believed them all, if it was only to spite the doctor for having received her intelligence so uncourteously. Peter de Groodt matched them with many a wonderful legend of the times of the Dutch dynasty, and of the Devil's Stepping-stones; and of the pirate hanged at Gibbet Island, that continued to swing there at night long after the gallows was taken down; and of the ghost of the unfortunate Governor Leisler, hanged for treason, which haunted the old fort and the government

173

house. The gossiping knot dispersed, each charged with direful intelligence. In a little time the whole town was in a buzz with tales about the haunted house. Some said that Claus Hopper had seen the devil, while others hinted that the house was haunted by the ghosts of some of the patients whom the doctor had physicked out of the world, and that was the reason why he did not venture to live in it himself.

All this put the little doctor in a terrible fume. He threatened vengeance on any one who should affect the value of his property by exciting popular prejudices. He complained loudly of thus being in a manner dispossessed of his territories by mere bugbears; but he secretly determined to have the house exorcised by the Dominie. Great was his relief, therefore, when in the midst of his perplexities, Dolph stepped forward and undertook to garrison the haunted house. The youngster had been listening to all the stories of Claus Hopper and Peter de Groodt: he was fond of adventure, he loved the marvellous, and his imagination had become quite excited by these tales of wonder. Besides, he had led such an uncomfortable life at the doctor's, being subjected to the intolerable thraldom of early hours, that he was delighted at the prospect of having a house to himself, even though it should be a haunted one. His offer was eagerly accepted, and it was determined he should mount guard that very night. His only stipulation was, that the enterprise should be kept secret from his mother; for he knew the poor soul would not sleep a wink if she knew her son was waging war with the powers of darkness.

When night came on he set out on this perilous expedition.

The old black cook, his only friend in the household, had provided him with a little mess for supper, and a rushlight; and she tied round his neck an amulet, given her by an African conjurer, as a charm against evil spirits. Dolph was escorted on his way by the doctor and Peter de Groodt, who had agreed to accompany him to the house, and to see him safe lodged. The night was overcast, and it was very dark when they arrived at the grounds which surrounded the mansion. The sexton led the way with the lantern. As they walked along the avenue of acacias, the fitful light, catching from bush to bush, and tree to tree, often startled the doughty Peter, and made him fall back upon his followers; and the doctor grappled still closer hold of Dolph's arm, observing that the ground was very slippery and uneven. At one time they were nearly put to a total rout by a bat, which came flitting about the lantern; and the notes of the insects from the trees and the frogs from a neighboring pond, formed a most drowsy and doleful concert. The front door of the mansion opened with a grating sound that made the doctor turn pale. They entered a tolerably large hall, such as is common in American country houses and which serves for a sitting-room in warm weather. From this they went up a wide staircase, that groaned and creaked as they trod, every step making its particular note, like the key of a harpsichord. This led to another hall on the second story, whence they entered the room where Dolph was to sleep. It was large, and scantily furnished; the shutters were closed; but as they were much broken, there was no want of a circulation of air. It appeared to have been that sacred chamber, known among Dutch housewives by the name of " the best bedroom "; which is the best furnished room in the house, but in which scarce anybody is ever permitted to sleep. Its splendor, however, was all at an end. There were a few broken articles of furniture about the room, and in the centre stood a heavy deal table and a large arm-chair, both of which had the look of being coeval with the mansion. The fire-place was wide, and had been faced with Dutch tiles, representing Scripture stories; but some of them had fallen out of their places, and lay scattered about the hearth. The sexton lit the rushlight; and the doctor, looking fearfully about the room, was just exhorting Dolph to be of good cheer, and to pluck up a stout heart, when a noise in the chimney, like voices and struggling, struck a sudden panic into the sexton. He took to his heels with the lantern; the doctor followed hard after him; the stairs groaned and creaked as they hurried down, increasing their agitation and speed by its noise. The front door slammed after them; and Dolph heard them scrabbling down the avenue, till the sound of their feet was lost in the distance.

Being now left to himself, he secured the front door by a strong bolt and bar; and having seen that the other entrances were fastened, returned to his desolate chamber. Having made his supper from the basket which the good old cook had provided, he locked the chamber door, and retired to rest on a mattress in one corner. The night was calm and still; and nothing broke upon the profound quiet but the lonely chirping of a cricket from the chimney of a distant chamber. The rushlight, which stood in the centre of the deal table, shed a feeble yellow ray, dimly illumining the chamber, and making uncouth shapes and shadows on the walls, from the clothes which Dolph had thrown over a chair.

With all his boldness of heart, there was something subduing in this desolate scene; and he felt his spirits flag within him, as he lay on his hard bed and gazed about the room. By and by he thought he heard a sound as of some one walking below stairs. He listened, and distinctly heard a step on the great staircase. It approached solemnly and slowly, tramp — tramp — tramp! It was evidently the tread of some heavy personage; and yet how could he have got into the house without making a noise? He had examined all the fastenings, and was certain that every entrance was secure. Still the steps advanced, tramp — tramp — tramp! It was evident that the person approaching could not be a robber, the step was too loud and

177

deliberate; a robber would either be stealthy or precipitate. And now the footsteps had ascended the staircase; they were slowly advancing along the passage, resounding through the silent and empty apartments. The door, which had been locked on the inside, slowly swung open, as if self-moved. The footsteps entered the room; but no one was to be seen. They passed slowly and audibly across it, tramp — tramp — tramp! but whatever made the sound was invisible. Dolph rubbed his eyes, and stared about him; he could see to every part of the dimly lighted chamber; all was vacant; yet still he heard those mysterious footsteps, solemnly walking about the chamber. They ceased, and all was dead silence. There was something more appalling in this invisible visitation than there would have been in anything that addressed itself to the eyesight. It was awfully vague and indefinite. He felt his heart beat against his ribs; a cold sweat broke out upon his forehead; he lay for some time in a state of violent agitation: nothing, however, occurred to increase his alarm. His light gradually burnt down into the socket, and he fell asleep. When he awoke it was broad daylight; the sun was peering through the cracks of the window-shutters, and the birds were merrily singing about the house. The bright cheery day soon put to flight all the terrors of the preceding night. Dolph laughed, or rather tried to laugh, at all that had passed, and endeavored to persuade himself that it was a mere freak of the imagination, conjured up by the stories he had heard; but he was a little puzzled to find the door of his room locked on the inside, notwithstanding that he had positively seen it swing open as the footsteps had entered. He returned to town in a state of considerable perplexity; but he determined to say nothing on the subject, until his doubts were either confirmed or removed by another night's watching.

The next night Dolph repeated his vigil. He now entered the house with some trepidation. He was particular in examining the fastenings of all the doors, and securing them well. He locked the door of his chamber, and placed a chair against it; then having despatched his supper, he threw himself on his mattress and endeavored to sleep. It was all in vain; a thousand crowding fancies kept him waking. The time slowly dragged on, as if minutes were spinning themselves out into hours. As the night advanced, he grew more and more nervous; and he almost started from his couch when he heard the mysterious footstep again on the staircase. Up it came, as before, solemnly and slowly, tramp — tramp — tramp! It approached along the passage; the door again swung open, as if there had been neither lock nor impediment, and a strange looking figure stalked into the room. It was an elderly man, large and robust, clothed in the old Flemish fashion. He had on a kind of short cloak, with a garment under it, belted round the waist; trunk-hose, with great bunches or bows at the knees; and a pair of russet boots, very large at top, and standing widely from his legs. His hat was broad and slouched, with a feather trailing over one side. His iron-gray hair hung in thick masses on his neck; and he had a short grizzled beard. He walked slowly round the room, as if examining that all was safe; then, hanging his hat on a peg beside the door, he sat down in the elbow-chair, and, leaning his elbow on the table, fixed his eyes on Dolph with an unmoving and deadening stare.

Dolph was not naturally a coward; but he had been brought up in an implicit belief in ghosts and goblins, and as he looked at this strange personage, with his uncouth garb, his pale visage, his grizzly beard, and his fixed, staring, fishlike eye, his teeth began to chatter, his hair to rise on his head, and a cold sweat to break out all over his body. How long he remained in this situation he could not tell, for he was like one fascinated. He could not take his gaze off from the spectre; but lay staring at him, with his whole intellect absorbed in the contemplation. The old man remained seated behind the table, without stirring, or turning an eye, always keeping a dead steady glare upon Dolph. At length the household cock, from a neighboring farm, clapped his wings, and gave a loud cheerful crow that rung over the fields. At the sound the old man slowly rose, and took down his hat from the peg; the door opened, and closed after him; he was heard to go slowly down the staircase, tramp — tramp — tramp! — and when he had got to the bottom, all was again silent. Dolph lay and listened earnestly; counted every footfall; listened, and listened, if the steps should return, until, exhausted by watching and agitation, he fell into a troubled sleep.

Daylight again brought fresh courage and assurance. He would fain have considered all that had passed as a mere dream; yet there stood the chair in which the unknown had seated himself; there was the table on which he had leaned; there was the peg on which he had hung his hat; and there was

180

the door, locked precisely as he himself had locked it, with the chair placed against it. He hastened down-stairs and examined the doors and windows; all were exactly in the same state in which he had left them, and there was no apparent way by which any being could have entered and left the house, without leaving some trace behind. " Pooh! " said Dolph to himself, " it was all a dream; " — but it would not do. The more he endeavored to shake the scene off from his mind, the more it haunted him.

Though he persisted in a strict silence as to all that he had seen or heard, yet his looks betrayed the uncomfortable night that he had passed. It was evident that there was something wonderful hidden under this mysterious reserve. The doctor took him into the study, locked the door, and sought to have a full and confidential communication; but he could get nothing out of him. Frau Ilsy took him aside into the pantry, but to as little purpose; and Peter de Groodt held him by the button for a full hour, in the churchyard, the very place to get at the bottom of a ghost story, but came off not a whit wiser than the rest. It is always the case, however, that one truth concealed makes a dozen current lies. It is like a guinea locked up in a bank, that has a dozen paper representatives. Before the day was over, the neighborhood was full of reports. Some said that Dolph Heyliger watched in the haunted house, with pistols loaded with silver bullets; others, that he had a long talk with a spectre without a head; others, that Doctor Knipperhausen and the sexton had been hunted down the Bowery lane, and quite into town, by a legion of ghosts of their customers.

Some shook their heads, and thought it a shame the doctor should put Dolph to pass the night alone in that dismal house, where he might be spirited away no one knew whither; while others observed, with a shrug, that if the devil did carry off the youngster, it would be but taking his own.

These rumors at length reached the ears of the good Dame Heyliger, and, as may be supposed, threw her into a terrible alarm. For her son to have opposed himself to danger from living foes would have been nothing so dreadful in her eyes, as to dare alone the terrors of the haunted house. She hastened to the doctor's, and passed a great part of the day in attempting to dissuade Dolph from repeating his vigil; she told him a score of tales, which her gossiping friends had just related to her, of persons who had been carried off when watching alone in old ruinous houses. It was all to no effect. Dolph's pride, as well as curiosity, was piqued. He endeavored to calm the apprehensions of his mother, and to assure her that there was no truth in all the rumors she had heard; she looked at him dubiously and shook her head; but finding his determination was not to be shaken, she brought him a little thick Dutch Bible, with brass clasps, to take with him, as a sword wherewith to fight the powers of darkness; and, lest that might not be sufficient, the housekeeper gave him the Heidelberg catechism by way of dagger.

The next night, therefore, Dolph took up his quarters for the third time in the old mansion. Towards midnight, when everything was still, the same sound echoed through the empty halls, tramp — tramp — tramp! The stairs were again ascended; the door again swung open; the old man entered; walked round the room; hung up his hat, and seated himself by the table. The same fear and trembling came over poor Dolph, though not in so violent a degree. He lay in the same way, motionless and fascinated, staring at the figure, which regarded him as before, with a dead, fixed, chilling gaze. In this way they remained for a long time, till, by degrees, Dolph's courage began gradually to revive. Whether alive or dead, this being had certainly some object in his visitation; and he recollected to have heard it said, spirits have no power to speak until spoken to. Summoning up resolution, therefore, and making two or three attempts, before he could get his parched tongue in motion, he addressed the unknown and demanded to know what was the motive of his visit.

No sooner had he finished, than the old man rose, took down his hat, the door opened, and he went out, looking back upon Dolph just as he crossed the threshold, as if expecting him to follow. The youngster did not hesitate an instant. He took the candle in his hand and the Bible under his arm, and obeyed the tacit invitation. The candle emitted a feeble, uncertain ray, but still he could see the figure before him slowly descend the stairs. He followed trembling. When it had reached the bottom of the stairs, it turned through the hall towards the back door of the mansion. Dolph held the light over the balustrades; but, in his eagerness to catch a sign of the unknown, he flared his feeble taper so suddenly, that it went out. Still there was sufficient light from the pale moonbeams, that fell

184

through a narrow window, to give him an indistinct view of the figure near the door. He followed, therefore, down-stairs, and turned towards the place; but when he arrived there the unknown had disappeared. The door remained fast barred and bolted; there was no other mode of exit, yet the being, whatever he might be, was gone. He unfastened the door, and looked out into the fields. It was a hazy, moonlight night, so that the eye could distinguish objects at some distance. He thought he saw the unknown in a footpath which led from the door. He was not mistaken; but how had he got out of the house? He did not pause to think, but followed on. The old man proceeded at a measured pace, without looking about him, his footsteps sounding on the hard ground. He passed through the orchard of apple-trees, always keeping the footpath. It led to a well, situated in a little hollow, which had supplied the farm with water. Just at this well Dolph lost sight of him. He rubbed his eyes and looked again; but nothing was to be seen of the unknown. He reached the well, but nobody was there. All the surrounding ground was open and clear; there was no bush nor hiding-place. He looked down the well, and saw, at a great depth, the reflection of the sky in the still water. After remaining here for some time, without seeing or hearing anything more of his mysterious conductor, he returned to the house, full of awe and wonder. He bolted the door, groped his way back to bed, and it was long before he could compose himself to sleep.

His dreams were strange and troubled. He thought he was following the old man along the side of a great river, until they came to a vessel on the point of sailing, and that his conductor led him on board and vanished. He remembered the commander of the vessel, a short, swarthy man, with crisped black hair, blind of one eye, and lame of one leg; but the rest of his dream was very confused. Sometimes he was sailing, sometimes on shore; now amidst storms and tempests, and now wandering quietly in unknown streets. The figure of the old man was strangely mingled with the incidents of the dream, and the whole distinctly wound up by his finding himself on board the vessel again, returning home, with a great bag of money!

When he woke, the gray, cool light of dawn was streaking the horizon, and the cocks passing the reveille from farm to farm throughout the country. He rose more harassed and perplexed than ever. He was singularly confounded by all that he had seen and dreamt, and began to doubt whether his mind

186

was not affected, and whether all that passing in his thoughts might not be mere feverish fantasy. In his present state of mind, he did not feel disposed to return immediately to the doctor's and undergo the cross-questioning of the household. He made a scanty breakfast, therefore, on the remains of the last night's provisions, and then wandered out into the fields to meditate on all that had befallen him. Lost in thought, he rambled about, gradually approaching the town, until the morning was far advanced, when he was aroused by a hurry and bustle around him. He found himself near the water's edge, in a throng of people, hurrying to a pier, where was a vessel ready to make sail. He was unconsciously carried along by the impulse of the crowd, and found that it was a sloop, on the point of sailing up the Hudson to Albany. There was much leave-taking, and kissing of old women and children, and great activity in carrying on board baskets of bread and cakes, and provisions of all kinds, notwithstanding the mighty joints of meat that dangled over the stern; for a voyage to Albany was an expedition of great moment in those days. The commander of the sloop was hurrying about, giving a world of orders, which were not very strictly attended to; one man being busy in lighting his pipe, and another in sharpening his snicker-snee.

The appearance of the commander suddenly caught Dolph's attention. He was short and swarthy, with crisped black hair; blind of one eye, and lame of one leg — the very commander that he had seen in his dream! Surprised and aroused, he considered the scene more attentively, and recalled still further traces of his dream: the appearance of the vessel, of the river, and of images, a variety of other objects accorded with the imperfect images vaguely rising to recollection.

As he stood musing on these circumstances, the captain suddenly called out to him in Dutch: " Step on board, young man, or you'll be left behind! " He was startled by the summons; he saw that the sloop was cast loose, and was actually moving from the pier. It seemed as if he was actuated by some irresistible impulse; he sprang upon the deck, and the next moment the sloop was hurried off by the wind and tide. Dolph's thoughts and feelings were all in tumult and confusion. He had been strongly worked upon by the events which had recently befallen him, and could not but think there was some connection between his present situation and his last night's dream. He felt as if under supernatural influence, and tried to assure himself with an old and favorite maxim of his, that " one way or other all would turn out for the best." He felt himself launched strangely and suddenly on the world, and under full way to explore the regions of wonder that lay up this mighty river and beyond those blue mountains which had bounded his horizon since childhood. While he was lost in this whirl of thought, the sails strained to the breeze; the shores seemed to hurry away behind him; and before he perfectly recovered his self-possession, the sloop was ploughing her way past Spiking-Devil and Yonkers, and the tallest chimney of the Manhattoes had faded from his sight.

In the second day of the voyage they came to the highlands. It was the latter part of a calm, sultry day that they floated gently with the tide between these stern mountains. There was that perfect quiet which prevails over nature in the languor of summer heat; the turning of a plank, or the accidental falling of an oar on deck, was echoed from the mountain-side, and reverberated along the shores; and if by chance the captain gave a shout of command, there were airy tongues which mocked it from every cliff.

To the left the Dunderberg reared its woody precipices, height over height, forest over forest, away into the deep summer sky. To the right, strutted forth the bold promontory of Antony's Nose, with a solitary eagle wheeling about it; while beyond, mountain succeeded to mountain, until they seemed to lock their arms together, and confine this mighty river in their embraces.

And now muttering peals of thunder were faintly heard rolling behind the mountains. The river, hitherto still and glassy, reflecting pictures of the sky and land, now showed a dark ripple at a distance, as the breeze came creeping up it. The fish-hawks wheeled and screamed, and sought their nests on the high dry trees. The crows flew clamorously to the crevices of the rocks, and all nature seemed conscious of the approaching thunder-gust.

The clouds rolled in volumes over the mountain-tops; their summits still bright and snowy, but the lower parts of an inky blackness. The rain began to patter down in broad and scattered drops; the wind freshened, and curled up the waves. At length it seemed as if the bellying clouds were torn open by the mountain-tops, and complete torrents of rain came rattling down. The lightning leaped from cloud to cloud, and streamed quivering against the rocks, splitting and rending the stoutest forest trees. The thunder burst in tremendous explosions; the peals were echoed from mountain to mountain; they crashed upon Dunderberg and rolled up the long defile of the highlands, each headland making a new echo, until old Bull Hill seemed to bellow back the storm.

For a time the scudding rack and mist, and the sheeted rain, almost hid the landscape from the sight. There was a fearful gloom, illumined still more fearfully by the streams of lightning which glittered among the raindrops. Never had Dolph beheld such an absolute warring of the elements; it seemed as if the storm was tearing and rending its way through this mountain defile, and had brought all the artillery of heaven into action.

The vessel was hurried on by the increasing wind, until she came to where the river makes a sudden bend, the only one in the whole course of its majestic career.[1] Just as they turned the point, a violent flaw of wind came sweeping down a mountain gully, bending the forest before it and in a moment, lashing up the river into white froth and foam. The captain saw the danger and cried out to lower the sail. Before the order could be obeyed, the flaw struck the sloop, and threw her on her beam ends. Everything now was fright and confusion: the flapping of the sails, the whistling and rushing of the wind, the bawling of the captain and crew, the shrieking of the passengers, all mingled with the rolling and bellowing of the thunder. In the midst of the uproar the sloop righted; at

[1] This must have been the bend at West Point.

the same time the mainsail shifted, the boom came sweeping the quarter-deck, and Dolph, who was gazing unguardedly at the clouds, found himself, in a moment, floundering in the river.

For once in his life one of his idle accomplishments was of use to him. The many truant hours he had devoted to sporting in the Hudson had made him an expert swimmer. Yet with all his strength and skill he found great difficulty in reaching the shore. His disappearance from the deck had not been noticed by the crew, who were all occupied by their own danger. The sloop was driven along with inconceivable rapidity. She had hard work to weather a long promontory on the eastern shore, round which the river turned, and which completely shut her from Dolph's view.

It was on a point of the western shore that he landed and, scrambling up the rocks, threw himself, faint and exhausted, at the foot of a tree. By degrees the thunder-gust passed over. Dolph rose, and sought about to see if any path led from the shore, but all was savage and trackless. The rocks were piled upon each other; great trunks of trees lay shattered about, as they had been blown down by the strong winds which draw through these mountains, or had fallen through age. The rocks, too, were overhung with wild vines and briers, which completely matted themselves together, and opposed a barrier to all ingress; every movement that he made shook down a shower from the dripping foliage. He attempted to scale one of these almost perpendicular heights; but, though strong and agile, he found it a Herculean undertaking. Often he was supported merely by crumbling projections of the rock, and sometimes he clung to roots and branches of trees, and hung almost suspended in the air. The wood-pigeon came cleaving his whistling flight by him, and the eagle screamed from the brow of the impending cliff. As he was thus clambering, he was on the point of seizing hold of a shrub to aid his ascent, when something rustled among the leaves, and he saw a snake quivering along like lightning, almost from under his hand. It coiled itself up immediately, in an attitude of defiance, with flattened head, distended jaws, and quickly vibrating tongue, that played like a little flame about its mouth. Dolph's heart turned faint within him, and he had well-nigh let go his hold and tumbled down the precipice. The serpent stood on the defensive but for an instant; and finding there was no attack, glided away into a cleft of the rock. Dolph's eye followed it with fearful intensity, and saw a nest of adders, knotted and writhing and hissing in the chasm. He hastened with all speed from so frightful a neighborhood. His imagination, full of this new horror, saw an adder in every curling vine, and heard the tail of a rattlesnake in every dry leaf that rustled.

At length he succeeded in scrambling to the summit of a precipice; but it was covered by a dense forest. Wherever he could gain a lookout between trees, he beheld heights and cliffs, one rising beyond another, until huge mountains overtopped the whole. There were no signs of cultivation; no smoke curling among the trees to indicate a human residence. Everything was wild and solitary. As he was standing on the edge of a precipice overlooking a deep ravine fringed with trees, his feet detached a great fragment of rock; it fell, crashing its way through the tree-tops, down into the chasm. A loud whoop, or rather yell, issued from the bottom of the glen; the moment after there was a report of a gun; and a ball came whistling over his head, cutting the twigs and leaves, and burying itself deep in the bark of a chestnut tree.

Dolph did not wait for a second shot, but made a precipitate retreat; fearing every moment to hear the enemy in pursuit. He succeeded, however, in returning unmolested to the shore, and determined to penetrate no farther into a country so beset with savage perils.

He sat himself down, dripping, on a stone. What was to be done? where was he to shelter himself? The birds were seeking their nests, the bat began to flit about in the twilight, and the night-hawk, soaring high in the heaven, seemed to be calling out the stars. Night gradually closed in, and wrapped everything in gloom; and though it was the latter part of summer, the breeze stealing along the river and among these dripping forests was chilly and penetrating, especially to a half-drowned man.

As he sat drooping and despondent in this comfortless condition, he perceived a light gleaming through the trees near the shore, where the winding of the river made a deep bay. With extreme difficulty he made his way toward the light, along ledges of rocks, down which he was in danger of sliding into the river, and over great trunks of fallen trees. At length he came to the brow of a rock overhanging a small dell, whence the light proceeded. It was from a fire at the foot of a great tree in the midst of a grassy plat among the rocks. The fire cast up a red glare among the gray crags and impending trees; leaving chasms of deep gloom. Two figures were moving about the fire, and others squatted before it. As they were between him and the light, they were in complete shadow; but one of them happening to move round to the opposite side, Dolph was startled at perceiving, by the glare falling on painted features and glittering on silver ornaments, that he was an Indian. He now looked more narrowly, and saw guns leaning against a tree, and a dead body lying on the ground. Here was the very foe that had fired at him from the glen. He endeavored to retreat quietly, not caring to intrust himself to these half-human beings in so savage and lonely a place. It was too late; the Indian, with that eagle quickness of eye so remarkable in his race, perceived something stirring among the bushes on the rock; he seized one of the guns that leaned against the tree; one moment more, and Dolph might have had his passion for adventure cured by a bullet. He hallooed loudly, with the Indian salutation of friendship; the whole party sprang upon their feet; the salutation was returned, and the straggler was invited to join them at the fire.

On approaching, he found, to his consolation, the party was composed of white men as well as Indians. One, evidently the principal personage, or commander, was seated on a trunk of a tree before the fire. He was a large, stout man, somewhat advanced in life, but hale and hearty. His face was bronzed almost to the color of an Indian's; he had strong but rather jovial features, an aquiline nose, and a mouth shaped like a mastiff's. His face was half thrown in shade by a broad hat, with a buck's tail in it. His gray hair hung short on his neck. He wore a hunting-frock, with Indian leggins, and moccasins, and a tomahawk in the broad wampum-belt round his waist. As Dolph caught a distinct view of his person and features, something reminded him of the old man of the haunted house. The man before him, however, was different in dress and age; he was more cheery too in aspect, and it was hard to find where the vague resemblance lay; but a resemblance there certainly was. Dolph felt some degree of awe in approaching him; but was assured by a frank, hearty welcome. He was still further encouraged by perceiving that the dead body, which had caused him some alarm, was that of a deer; and his satisfaction was complete in discerning by savory steams from a kettle, suspended by a hooked stick over the fire, that there was a part cooking for the evening's repast.

He had, in fact, fallen in with a rambling hunting-party, such as often took place in those days among the settlers along the river. The hunter is always hospitable; and nothing makes men more social and unceremonious than meeting in the wilderness. The commander of the party poured out a dram of cheering liquor, which he gave him with a merry leer, to warm his heart; and ordered one of his followers to fetch some garments from a pinnace, moored in a cove close by, while those in which our hero was dripping might be dried before the fire.

Dolph found, as he had suspected, that the shot from the glen, which had come so near giving him his quietus when on the precipice, was from the party before him. He had nearly crushed one of them by the fragments of rock which he had

195

detached; and the jovial old hunter, in the broad hat and buck-tail, had fired at the place where he saw the bushes move, supposing it to be the sound of some wild animal. He laughed heartily at the blunder, it being what is considered an exceeding good joke among hunters: " But faith, my lad," said he, " if I had but caught a glimpse of you to take sight at, you would have followed the rock. Antony Vander Heyden is seldom known to miss his aim." The commander in the broad hat and hunting-frock was no less a personage than the Heer Antony Vander Heyden, of Albany, of whom Dolph had many a time heard. He was, in fact, the hero of many a story, his singular humors and whimsical habits being matters of wonder to his quiet Dutch neighbors. As he was a man of property, having had a father before him from whom he inherited large tracts of wild land, and whole barrels full of wampum, he could indulge his humors without control. Instead of staying quietly at home, eating and drinking at regular mealtimes, amusing himself by smoking his pipe on the bench before the door, and then turning into a comfortable bed at night, he delighted in all kinds of rough, wild expeditions; never so happy as when on a hunting-party in the wilderness, sleeping under trees or bark sheds, or cruising down the river, or on some woodland lake, fishing and fowling, and living the Lord knows how.

He was a great friend to Indians, and to an Indian mode of life; which he considered true natural liberty and manly enjoyment. When at home he had always several Indian hangers-on who loitered about his house, sleeping like hounds in the sunshine; or preparing hunting and fishing tackle for

ANTONY VANDER HEYDEN

some new expedition; or shooting at marks with bows and arrows.

Over these vagrant beings Heer Antony had as perfect command as a huntsman over his pack. As he was a rich man, no one ventured to thwart his humors; indeed, his hearty, joyous manner made him universally popular. He would troll a Dutch song as he tramped along the street; hail every one a mile off, and when he entered a house, would slap the good man familiarly on the back, shake him by the hand till he roared, and kiss his wife and daughter before his face, — in short, there was no pride nor ill humor about Heer Antony.

Besides his Indian hangers-on, he had three or four humble friends among the white men, who looked up to him as a patron, and had the run of his kitchen, and the favor of being taken with him occasionally on his expeditions. With a medley of such retainers he was at present on a cruise along the shores of the Hudson, in a pinnace kept for his own recreation. There were two white men with him, dressed partly in the Indian style, with moccasins and hunting-shirts; the rest of his crew consisted of four favorite Indians. They had been prowling about the river, without any definite object, until they found themselves in the highlands; where they had passed two or three days, hunting the deer which still lingered among these mountains.

"It is lucky for you, young man," said Antony Vander Heyden, "that you happened to be knocked overboard to-day, as to-morrow morning we start early on our return homewards; and you might then have looked in vain for a meal among the mountains — but come, lads, stir about! stir about! Let's see what prog we have for supper; the kettle has boiled long enough; my stomach cries cupboard; and I'll warrant our guest is in no mood to dally with his trencher.

There was a bustle now in the little encampment; one took off the kettle and turned a part of the contents into a huge wooden bowl. Another prepared a flat rock for a table; while a third brought various utensils from the pinnace; Heer Antony himself brought a flask or two of precious liquor from his own private locker; knowing his boon companions too well to trust any of them with the key.

A rude but hearty repast was soon spread; consisting of venison smoking from the kettle, with cold bacon, boiled Indian corn, and mighty loaves of good brown household bread. Never had Dolph made a more delicious repast; and when he had washed it down with two or three draughts from the Heer Antony's flask, and felt the jolly liquor sending its warmth through his veins, and glowing round his very heart, he would not have changed his situation, no, not with the governor of the province.

The Heer Antony, too, grew chirping and joyous; told half a dozen fat stories, at which his white followers laughed immoderately, though the Indians, as usual, maintained an invincible gravity.

" This is your true life, my boy! " said he, slapping Dolph on the shoulder; " a man is never a man till he can defy wind and weather, range woods and wilds, sleep under a tree, and live on basswood leaves! "

And then would he sing a stave or two of a Dutch drinking-song, swaying a short swab Dutch bottle in his hand, while his myrmidons would join in the chorus, until the woods echoed again; — as the good old song has it,

> *" They all with a shout made the elements ring*
> *So soon as the office was o'er,*
> *To feasting they went, with true merriment,*
> *And tippled strong liquor gillore."*

In the midst of his joviality, however, Heer Antony did not lose sight of discretion. Though he pushed the bottle without reserve to Dolph, he always took care to help his followers himself, knowing the beings he had to deal with; and was particular in granting but a moderate allowance to the Indians. The repast being ended, the Indians having drunk their liquor, and smoked their pipes, now wrapped themselves in their blankets, stretched themselves on the ground, with their feet to the fire, and soon fell asleep, like so many tired hounds. The rest of the party remained chatting before the fire. The conversation gradually moderated from the hilarity of supper-time, and turned upon hunting-adventures, and exploits and perils in the wilderness. As the sturdy bushbeater sat in a twisted root of a tree, that served him for an arm-chair, dealing forth these wild stories, with the fire gleaming on his strongly marked visage, Dolph was again repeatedly perplexed by something that reminded him of the phantom of the haunted house.

The circumstance of Dolph's falling overboard led to the relation of divers disasters and singular mishaps that had befallen voyagers on this great river, particularly in the earlier periods of colonial history; most of which the Heer deliberately attributed to supernatural causes. Dolph stared at this suggestion; but the old gentleman assured him it was very currently believed by the settlers along the river, that these highlands were under the dominion of supernatural and mischievous beings, which seemed to have taken some pique against the Dutch colonists in the early time of the settlement. In consequence of this, they have ever taken particular delight in venting their spleen, and indulging their humors upon the Dutch skippers; bothering them with flaws, head-winds, countercurrents, and all kinds of impediments, insomuch, that a Dutch navigator was always obliged to be exceedingly wary and deliberate in his proceedings; to come to anchor at dusk; to drop his peak, or take in sail, whenever he saw a swag-bellied cloud rolling over the mountains; in short, to take so many precautions, that he was often apt to be an incredible time in toiling up the river.

FOREST LEGENDS

Some, he said, believed these mischievous powers of the air to be the evil spirits conjured up by the Indian wizards, in the early times of the province, to revenge themselves on the strangers who had dispossessed them of their country. They even attributed to their incantations the misadventure which befell the renowned Hendrick Hudson, when he sailed so gallantly up this river in quest of a northwest passage and, as he thought, ran his ship aground; which they affirm was nothing more nor less than a spell of these same wizards, to prevent his getting to China in this direction.

The greater part, however, Heer Antony observed, accounted for all the extraordinary circumstances attending this river, and the perplexities of the skippers who navigated it, by the old legend of the Storm-ship which haunted Point-no-point. On finding Dolph to be utterly ignorant of this tradition, the Heer stared at him with surprise, and wondered where he had passed his life, to be uninformed on so important a point of history. Giving a stir to the fire, that sent up its sparks among the trees like a little volcano, he adjusted himself comfortably in his root of a tree, and throwing back his head, and closing his eyes for a few moments, to summon up his recollection, he related the following legend.

THE STORM-SHIP

The Storm-Ship

IN THE golden age of the province of the New Netherlands, when under the sway of Wouter Van Twiller, otherwise called the Doubter, the people of the Manhattoes were alarmed one sultry afternoon, just about the time of the summer solstice, by a tremendous storm of thunder and lightning. The rain fell in such torrents as absolutely to spatter up and smoke along the ground. It seemed as if the thunder rattled and rolled over the very roofs of the houses; the lightning was seen to play about the church of St. Nicholas, and to strive three times, in vain, to strike its weather-cock. Garret Van Horne's new chimney was split almost from top to bottom; Doffue Mildeberger was struck speechless from his baldfaced mare, just as he was riding into town. It was one of those unparalleled storms which only happen once within the memory of that venerable personage known in all towns by the appellation of " the oldest inhabitant."

Great was the terror of the good old women of the Manhattoes. They gathered their children together, and took refuge in the cellars; after having hung a shoe on the iron point of every bedpost, lest it should attract the lightning. At length the storm abated; the thunder sank into a growl, and the setting sun, breaking from under the fringed borders of the clouds, made the broad bosom of the bay to gleam like a sea of molten gold.

205

The word was given from the fort that a ship was standing up the bay. It passed from mouth to mouth, and street to street, and soon put the little capital in a bustle. The arrival of a ship, in those early times of the settlement, was an event of vast importance to the inhabitants. It brought them news from the old world, from the land of their birth from which they were so completely severed; to the yearly ship, too, they looked for their supply of luxuries, of finery, of comforts, and almost of necessaries. The good vrouw could not have her new cap nor new gown until the arrival of the ship; the artist waited for it for his tools, the burgomaster for his pipe and his supply of Hollands, the schoolboy for his top and marbles, and the lordly landholder for the bricks with which he was to build his new mansion. Thus every one, rich and poor, great and small, looked out for the arrival of the ship. It was the great yearly event of the town of New Amsterdam; and from one end of the year to the other, the ship — the ship — the ship — was the continual topic of conversation.

The news from the fort, therefore, brought all the populace down to the Battery, to behold the wished-for sight. It was not exactly the time when she had been expected to arrive, and the circumstance was a matter of some speculation. Many were the groups collected about the Battery. Here and there might be seen a burgomaster, of slow and pompous gravity, giving his opinion with great confidence to a crowd of old women and idle boys. At another place was a knot of old weather-beaten fellows, who had been seamen or fishermen in their times, and were great authorities on such occasions. These gave different opinions, and caused great disputes among their several adherents; but the man most looked up to, and followed and watched by the crowd, was Hans Van Pelt, an old Dutch sea-captain retired from service, the nautical oracle of the place. He reconnoitred the ship through an ancient telescope, covered with tarry canvas, hummed a Dutch tune to himself, and said nothing. A hum, however, from Hans Van Pelt, had always more weight with the public than a speech from another man.

In the meantime the ship became more distinct to the naked eye: she was a stout, round, Dutch-built vessel, with high bow and poop, and bearing Dutch colors. The evening sun gilded her bellying canvas, as she came riding over the long waving billows. The sentinel who had given notice of her approach, declared, that he first got sight of her when she was in the centre of the bay; and that she broke suddenly on his sight, just as if she had come out of the bosom of the black thunder-cloud. The bystanders looked at Hans Van Pelt, to see what he would say to this report; Hans Van Pelt screwed his mouth closer together, and said nothing; upon which some shook their heads, and others shrugged their shoulders.

The ship was now repeatedly hailed, but made no reply, and passing by the fort, stood on up the Hudson. A gun was brought to bear on her and, with some difficulty, loaded and fired by Hans Van Pelt, the garrison not being expert in artillery. The shot seemed absolutely to pass through the ship, and to skip along the water on the other side, but no notice was taken of it! What was strange, she had all her sails set, and sailed right against wind and tide, which were both down the river. Upon this Hans Van Pelt, who was likewise harbor-master, ordered his boat, and set off to board her; but after rowing two or three hours, he returned without success. Sometimes he would get within one or two hundred yards of her, and then, in a twinkling, she would be half a mile off. Some said it was because his oarsmen, who were rather pursy and short-winded, stopped every now and then to take breath, and spit on their hands; but this it is probable was a mere scandal. He got near enough, however, to see the crew; who were all dressed in the Dutch style, the officers in doublets and high hats and feathers. Not a word was spoken by any one on board; they stood as motionless as so many statues, and the ship seemed as if left to her own government. Thus she kept on, away up the river, lessening and lessening in the evening sunshine, until she faded from sight, like a little white cloud melting away in the summer sky.

The appearance of this ship threw the governor into one of the deepest doubts that ever beset him in the whole course of his administration. Fears were entertained for the security of the infant settlements on the river, lest this might be an enemy's ship in disguise, sent to take possession. The governor called together his council repeatedly to assist him with their conjectures. He sat in his chair of state, built of timber from the sacred forest of the Hague, smoking his long jasmin pipe, and listening to all that his counsellors had to say on a subject about which they knew nothing; but in spite of all the conjecturing of the sagest and oldest heads, the governor still continued to doubt.

Messengers were despatched to different places on the river; but they returned without any tidings — the ship had made no port. Day after day, and week after week, elapsed, but she never returned down the Hudson. As, however, the council seemed solicitous for intelligence, they had it in abundance. The captains of the sloops seldom arrived without bringing some report of having seen the strange ship at different parts of the river; sometimes near the Pallisadoes, sometimes off Croton Point, and sometimes in the highlands; but she never was reported as having been seen above the highlands. The crews of the sloops, it is true, generally differed among themselves in their accounts of these apparitions; but that may have arisen from the uncertain situations in which they saw her. Sometimes it was by the flashes of the thunder-storm lighting up a pitchy night, and giving glimpses of her careering across Tappaan Zee, or the wide waste of Haverstraw Bay. At one moment she would appear close upon them, as if likely to run them down, and would throw them into great bustle and alarm; but the next flash would show her far off, always sailing against the wind. Sometimes, in quiet moonlight nights, she would be seen under some high bluff of the highlands, all in deep shadow, excepting her top-sails glittering in the moonbeams; by the time, however, that the voyagers reached the place, no ship was to be seen; and when they had passed on for some distance, and looked back, behold! there she was again, with her topsails in the moonshine! Her appearance was always just after, or just before, or just in the midst of unruly weather; and she was known among the skippers and voyagers of the Hudson by the name of the *Storm-Ship.*

These reports perplexed the governor and his council more than ever; and it would be endless to repeat the conjectures and opinions uttered on the subject. Some quoted cases in point, of ships seen off the coast of New England, navigated by witches and goblins. Old Hans Van Pelt, who had been more than once to the Dutch colony at the Cape of Good Hope, insisted that this must be the flying Dutchman, which had so long haunted Table Bay; but being unable to make port, had now sought another harbor. Others suggested, that, if it really was a supernatural apparition, as there was every natural reason to believe, it might be Hendrick Hudson, and his crew of the *Half-Moon;* who, it was well known, had once run aground in the upper part of the river in seeking a northwest passage to China. This opinion had very little weight with the governor, but it passed current out of doors; for indeed it had already been reported, that Hendrick Hudson and his crew haunted the Kaatskill Mountains; and it appeared very reasonable to suppose, that his ship might infest the river where the enterprise was baffled, or that it might bear the shadowy crew to their periodical revels in the mountain.

Other events occurred to occupy the thoughts and doubts of the sage Wouter and his council, and the *Storm-Ship* ceased to be a subject of deliberation at the board. It continued, however, a matter of popular belief and marvellous anecdote through the whole time of the Dutch government, and particu-

larly just before the capture of New Amsterdam, and the subjugation of the province by the English squadron. About that time the *Storm-Ship* was repeatedly seen in the Tappaan Zee; and about Weehawk, and even down as far as Hoboken; and her appearance was supposed to be ominous of the approaching squall in public affairs, and the downfall of Dutch domination.

Since that time we have no authentic accounts of her; though it is said she still haunts the highlands, and cruises about Point-no-point. People who live along the river insist that they sometimes see her in summer moonlight; and that in a deep still midnight they have heard the chant of her crew. as if heaving the lead.

It is certain that strange things have been seen in these highlands in storms, which are considered as connected with the old story of the ship. The captains of the river craft talk of a little bulbous-bottomed Dutch goblin, in trunk-hose and sugar-loafed hat, with a speaking-trumpet in his hand, which they say keeps about the Dunderberg.[1] They declare that they have heard him, in stormy weather, in the midst of the turmoil, giving orders in Low Dutch for the piping up of a fresh gust of wind, or the rattling off of another thunder-clap. That sometimes he has been seen surrounded by a crew of little imps in broad breeches and short doublets; tumbling head-over-heels in the rack and mist, and playing a thousand gambols in the air; or buzzing like a swarm of flies about Antony's Nose; and that, at such times, the hurry-scurry of the storm was al-

[1] "The Thunder-Mountain," so called from its echoes.

ways greatest. One time a sloop, in passing by the Dunderberg, was overtaken by a thunder-gust, that came scouring round the mountain, and seemed to burst just over the vessel. Though tight and well ballasted, she labored dreadfully, and the water came over the gunwale. All the crew were amazed when it was discovered that there was a little white sugar-loaf hat on the mast-head, known at once to be the hat of the Heer of the Dunderberg. Nobody, however, dared to climb to the mast-head, and get rid of this terrible hat. The sloop continued laboring and rocking, as if she would have rolled her mast overboard, and seemed in continual danger either of upsetting or of running on shore. In this way she drove quite through the highlands, until she had passed Pollopol's Island, where, it is said, the jurisdiction of the Dunderberg potentate ceases. No sooner had she passed this bourn, than the little hat spun up into the air like a top, whirled up all the clouds into a vortex, and hurried them back to the summit of the Dunderberg; while the sloop righted herself, and sailed on as quietly as if in a mill-pond. Nothing saved her from utter wreck but the fortunate circumstances of having a horse-shoe nailed against the mast, — a wise precaution against evil spirits, since adopted by all the Dutch captains that navigate this haunted river.

There is another story told of this foul-weather urchin, by Skipper Daniel Ouselsticker, of Fishkill, who was never known to tell a lie. He declared, that, in a severe squall, he saw him seated astride of his bowsprit, riding the sloop ashore, full butt against Antony's Nose, and that he was exorcised by Dominie Van Gieson, of Esopus, who happened to be on board, and who sang the hymn of St. Nicholas; whereupon the goblin threw himself up in the air like a ball, and went off in a whirlwind, carrying away with him the nightcap of the Dominie's wife; which was discovered the next Sunday morning hanging on the weather-cock of Esopus church-steeple, at least forty miles off! Several events of this kind having taken place, the regular skippers of the river, for a long time, did not venture to pass the Dunderberg without lowering their peaks, out of homage to the Heer of the mountain; and it was observed that all such as paid this tribute of respect were suffered to pass unmolested.

"Such," said Antony Vander Heyden, "are a few of the stories written down by Selyne, the poet, concerning the *Storm-Ship,* — which he affirms to have brought a crew of mischievous imps into the province, from some old ghost-ridden country of Europe. I could give a host more, if necessary; for all the accidents that so often befall the river craft in the highlands are said to be tricks played off by these imps of the Dunderberg; but I see that you are nodding, so let us turn in for the night."

The moon had just raised her silver horns above the round back of Old Bull Hill, and lit up the gray rocks and shagged forests, and glittered on the waving bosom of the river. The night dew was falling, and the late gloomy mountains began to soften and put on a gray aërial tint in the dewy light. The hunters stirred the fire, and threw on fresh fuel to qualify the damp of the night air. They then prepared a bed of branches and dry leaves under a ledge of rocks for Dolph; while Antony Vander Heyden, wrapping himself in a huge coat of skins, stretched himself before the fire. It was some time, however, before Dolph could close his eyes. He lay contemplating the strange scene before him: the wild woods and rocks around; the fire throwing fitful gleams on the faces of the sleeping savages; and the Heer Antony, too, who so singularly reminded him of the nightly visitant to the haunted house. Now and then he heard the cry of some wild animal from the forest; or the hooting of the owl; or the notes of the whippoorwill, which seemed to abound among these solitudes; or the splash of a sturgeon, leaping out of the river and falling back full-length on its placid surface. His thoughts wandered to his poor old mother: what would she think of his mysterious disappearance — what anxiety and distress would she not suffer? This thought would continually intrude itself to mar his present enjoyment. It brought with it a feeling of pain and compunction, and he fell asleep with the tears yet standing in his eyes.

At an early hour of the next day, after a hearty morning's meal, the encampment broke up, and our adventurers embarked in the pinnace of Antony Vander Heyden. There being no wind for the sails, the Indians rowed her gently along, keeping time to a kind of chant of one of the white men. The day was serene and beautiful; the river without a wave; and as the vessel cleft the glassy water, it left a long undulating track behind. The crows, who had scented the hunters' banquet, were already gathering and hovering in the air, just where a column of thin, blue smoke, rising from among the trees showed the place of

216

their last night's quarters. As they coasted along the bases of the mountains, the Heer Antony pointed out to Dolph a bald eagle, the sovereign of these regions, who sat perched on a dry tree that projected over the river and, with eye turned upwards, seemed to be drinking in the splendor of the morning sun. Their approach disturbed the monarch's meditations. He first spread one wing, and then the other; balanced himself for a moment, and then, quitting his perch with dignified composure, wheeled slowly over their heads. Dolph snatched up a gun, and sent a whistling ball after him, that cut some of the feathers from his wing. The report of the gun leaped sharply from rock to rock, and awakened a thousand echoes. But the monarch of the air sailed calmly on, ascending higher and higher, and wheeling widely as he ascended, soaring up the green bosom of the woody mountain, until he disappeared over the brow of a beetling precipice. Dolph felt in a manner rebuked by this proud tranquillity, and almost reproached himself for having so wantonly insulted this majestic bird. Heer Antony told him, laughing, to remember that he was not yet out of the territories of the lord of the Dunderberg; and an old Indian shook his head, and observed, that there was bad luck in killing an eagle. The hunter, on the contrary, should always leave him a portion of his spoils.

When encamped by the water-side, some of the party would go into the woods and hunt; others would fish. Sometimes they would amuse themselves by shooting at a mark, by leaping, by running, by wrestling; and Dolph gained great favor in the eyes of Antony Vander Heyden, by his skill and adroitness in all these exercises, which the Heer considered as the highest of manly accomplishments.

Thus did they coast jollily on, choosing only the pleasant hours for voyaging; sometimes in the cool morning dawn, sometimes in the sober evening twilight, and sometimes when the moonshine spangled the crisp curling waves that whispered along the sides of their little bark. Never had Dolph felt so completely in his element; never had he met with anything so completely to his taste as this wild haphazard life. He was the very man to second Antony Vander Heyden in his rambling humors, and gained continually on his affections. The heart of the old bushwhacker yearned toward the young man, who seemed thus growing up in his own likeness; and as they approached to the end of their voyage, he could not help inquiring a little into his history. Dolph frankly told him his course of life, his severe medical studies, his little proficiency, and his very dubious prospects. The Heer was shocked to find that such amazing talents and accomplishments were to be cramped and buried under a doctor's wig. But to think that a young fellow like Dolph, of such wonderful abilities, who could shoot, fish, run, jump, ride, and wrestle, should be obliged to roll pills, and administer juleps for a living — 't was monstrous! He told Dolph never to despair, but to " throw physic to the dogs "; for a young fellow of his prodigious talents could never fail to make his way. " As you seem to have no acquaintance in Albany," said Heer Antony, " you shall go home with me, and remain under my roof until you can look about you; and in the meantime we can take an occasional bout at shooting and fishing, for it is a pity that such talents should lie idle."

Dolph, who was at the mercy of chance, was not hard to be persuaded.

On their arrival at Albany, the sight of Dolph's companion seemed to cause universal satisfaction. Many were the greetings at the river-side, and the salutations in the streets; the dogs bounded before him; the boys whooped as he passed; everybody seemed to know Antony Vander Heyden. Dolph followed on in silence, admiring the neatness of this worthy burgh; for in those days Albany was in all its glory, and inhabited almost exclusively by the descendants of the original Dutch settlers, not having as yet been discovered and colonized by the restless people of New England. Everything was quiet and orderly; everything was conducted calmly and leisurely; no hurry, no bustle, no struggling and scrambling for existence. The grass grew about the unpaved streets, and relieved the eye by its refreshing verdure. Tall sycamores or pendent willows shaded the houses, with caterpillars swinging in long silken strings from their branches; or moths, fluttering about like coxcombs, in joy at their gay transformation. The houses were built in the old Dutch style, with the gable-ends toward the street. The thrifty housewife was seated on a bench before her door, in close-crimped cap, bright-flowered gown, and white apron, busily employed in knitting. The husband smoked his pipe on the opposite bench; and the little pet negro girl, seated on the step at her mistress's feet, was industriously plying her needle. The swallows sported about the eaves, or skimmed along the streets,

219

and brought back some rich booty for their clamorous young; and the little housekeeping wren flew in and out of a Liliputian house, or an old hat nailed against the wall. The cows were coming home, lowing through the streets, to be milked at their owner's door; and if, perchance, there were any loiterers, some negro urchin, with a long goad, was gently urging them homewards.

As Dolph's companion passed on, he received a tranquil nod from the burghers, and a friendly word from their wives; all calling him familiarly by the name of Antony; for it was the custom in this stronghold of the patriarchs, where they had all grown up together from childhood, to call each other by the Christian name. The Heer did not pause to have his usual jokes with them, for he was impatient to reach his home. At length they arrived at his mansion. It was of some magnitude, in the Dutch style, with large iron figures on the gables, that gave the date of its erection, and showed that it had been built in the earliest times of the settlement.

The news of Heer Antony's arrival had preceded him, and the whole household was on the look-out. A crew of negroes, large and small, had collected in front of the house to receive him. The old, white-headed ones, who had grown gray in his service, grinned for joy, and made many awkward bows and grimaces, and the little ones capered about his knees. But the most happy being in the household was a little, plump, blooming lass, his only child, and the darling of his heart. She came bounding out of the house; but the sight of a strange young man with her father called up, for a moment, all the bashfulness

of a home-bred damsel. Dolph gazed at her with wonder and
delight; never had he seen, as he thought, anything so comely
in the shape of a woman. She was dressed in the good old
Dutch taste, with long stays, and full, short petticoats. Her
hair, turned up under a small round cap, displayed the fairness
of her forehead; she had fine blue, laughing eyes, a trim, slender waist, in a word, she was a little Dutch divinity; and Dolph,
who never stopped half-way in a new impulse, fell desperately
in love with her.

Dolph was now ushered into the house with a hearty welcome. In the interior was a mingled display of Heer Antony's
taste and habits, and of the opulence of his predecessors. The
chambers were furnished with good old mahogany; the beaufets
and cupboards glittered with embossed silver and painted
china. Over the parlor fireplace was, as usual, the family coat-
of-arms, painted and framed; above which was a long duck
fowling-piece, flanked by an Indian pouch and a powder-horn.
The room was decorated with many Indian articles, such as
pipes of peace, tomahawks, scalping-knives, hunting-pouches,
and belts of wampum; and there were various kinds of fishing-
tackle, and two or three fowling-pieces in the corners. The
household affairs seemed to be conducted, in some measure,
after the master's humors; corrected, perhaps, by a little quiet
management of the daughter's. There was a great degree of
patriarchal simplicity, and good-humored indulgence. The negroes came into the room without being called, merely to look
at their master, and hear of his adventures; they would stand
listening at the door until he had finished a story, and then go

off on a broad grin, to repeat it in the kitchen. A couple of pet negro children were playing about the floor with the dogs, and sharing with them their bread and butter. All the domestics looked hearty and happy; and when the table was set for the evening repast, the variety and abundance of good household luxuries bore testimony to the open-handed liberality of the Heer, and the notable housewifery of his daughter.

In the evening there dropped in several of the worthies of the place, the Van Renssellaers, and the Gansevoorts, and the Rosebooms, and others of Antony Vander Heyden's intimates, to hear an account of his expedition; for he was the Sinbad of Albany, and his exploits and adventures were favorite topics of conversation among the inhabitants. While these sat gossiping together about the door of the hall, and telling long twilight stories, Dolph was cosily seated, entertaining the daughter, on a window-bench. He had already got on intimate terms; for those were not times of false reserve and idle ceremony.

What Dolph whispered in her ear that long summer evening it is impossible to say; his words were so low and indistinct that they never reached the ear of the historian. In the meantime the visitors, one by one, departed; Antony Vander Heyden, who had fairly talked himself silent, sat nodding alone in his chair by the door, when he was suddenly aroused by a hearty salute with which Dolph Heyliger had unguardedly rounded off one of his periods and which echoed through the still chamber like the report of a pistol. The Heer started up, rubbed his eyes, called for lights, and observed that it was high time to go to bed; though, on parting for the night, he squeezed

Dolph heartily by the hand, looked kindly in his face, and shook his head knowingly; for the Heer well remembered what he himself had been at the youngster's age.

The chamber in which our hero was lodged was spacious, and panelled with oak. It was furnished with clothes-presses, and mighty chests of drawers, well waxed, and glittering with brass ornaments. These contained ample stock of family linen; for the Dutch housewives had always a laudable pride in showing off their household treasures to strangers.

Dolph's mind, however, was too full to take particular note of the objects around him; yet he could not help continually comparing the free, open-hearted cheeriness of this establishment with the starveling, sordid, joyless housekeeping at Doctor Knipperhausen's. Still, something marred the enjoyment: the idea that he must take leave of his hearty host and pretty hostess, and cast himself once more adrift upon the world. To linger here would be folly. He should only get deeper in love; and for a poor varlet, like himself, to aspire to the daughter of the great Heer Vander Heyden — it was madness to think of such a thing! The very kindness that the girl had shown towards him prompted him, on reflection, to hasten his departure; it would be a poor return for the frank hospitality of his host to entangle his daughter's heart in an injudicious attachment.

" This is a fine conclusion, truly, of my voyage," said he, as he almost buried himself in a sumptuous feather bed, and drew the fresh white sheets up to his chin. " Here am I, instead of finding a bag of money to carry home, launched in a strange place, with scarcely a stiver in my pocket; and, what is worse, have jumped ashore up to my very ears in love into the bargain. However," added he, after some pause, stretching himself, and turning himself in bed, " I'm in good quarters for the present, at least; so I'll e'en enjoy the present moment, and let the next take care of itself; I dare say all will work out, ' somehow or other,' for the best."

As he said these words, he reached out his hand to extinguish the candle, when he was suddenly struck with astonishment and dismay, for he thought he beheld the phantom of the haunted house, staring on him from a dusky part of the chamber. A second look reassured him, as he perceived that what he had taken for the spectre was, in fact, nothing but a Flemish portrait, hanging in a shadowy corner, just behind a clothespress. It was, however, the precise representation of his nightly visitor. The same cloak and belted jerkin, the same grizzled beard and fixed eye, the same broad slouched hat, with a feather hanging over one side. Dolph now called to mind the resemblance he had frequently remarked between his host and the old man of the haunted house; and was fully convinced they were in some way connected, and that some especial destiny had governed his voyage. He lay gazing on the portrait with almost as much awe as he had gazed on the ghostly original, until the shrill house-clock warned him of the lateness of the hour. He put out the light, but remained for a long time turning over these curious circumstances and coincidences in his mind, until he fell asleep. His dreams partook of the nature of his waking thoughts. He fancied that he still lay gazing on the picture, until, by degrees, it became animated; that the figure descended from the wall, and walked out of the room; that he followed it, and found himself by the well to which the old man pointed, smiled on him, and disappeared.

In the morning, when he waked, he found his host standing by his bedside, who gave him a hearty morning's salutation, and asked him how he had slept. Dolph answered cheerily; but took occasion to inquire about the portrait that hung against the wall. " Ah," said Heer Antony, " that's a portrait of old Killian Vander Spiegel, once a burgomaster of Amsterdam, who, on some popular troubles, abandoned Holland, and came over to the province during the government of Peter Stuyvesant. He was my ancestor by the mother's side, and an old miserly curmudgeon he was. When the English took possession of New Amsterdam, in 1664, he retired into the country. He fell into a melancholy, apprehending that his wealth would be taken from him and he come to beggary. He turned all his property into cash, and used to hide it away. He was for a year or two concealed in various places, fancying himself sought after by the English, to strip him of his wealth; and finally he was found dead in his bed one morning, without any one being able to discover where he had concealed the greater part of his money."

When his host had left the room, Dolph remained for some time lost in thought. His whole mind was occupied by what he had heard. Vander Spiegel was his mother's family name; and he recollected to have heard her speak of this very Killian Vander Spiegel as one of her ancestors. He had heard her say, too, that her father was Killian's rightful heir, only that the old man died without leaving anything to be inherited. It now appeared that Heer Antony was likewise a descendant, and perhaps an heir also, of this poor rich man; and that thus the Heyligers and the Vander Heydens were remotely connected. "What," thought he, "if, after all, this is the interpretation of my dream, that this is the way I am to make my fortune by this voyage to Albany, and that I am to find the old man's hidden wealth in the bottom of that well? But what an odd roundabout mode of communicating the matter! Why the plague could not the old goblin have told me about the well at once, without sending me all the way to Albany, to hear a story that was to send me all the way back again?"

These thoughts passed through his mind while he was dressing. He descended the stairs, full of perplexity, when the bright face of Marie Vander Heyden suddenly beamed in smiles upon him, and seemed to give him a clue to the whole mystery. "After all," thought he, "the old goblin is in the right. If I am to get his wealth, he means that I shall marry his pretty descendant; thus both branches of the family will again be united, and the property go on in the proper channel."

No sooner did this idea enter his head, than it carried conviction with it. He was now all impatience to hurry back and secure the treasure, which, he did not doubt, lay at the bottom of the well, and which he feared every moment might be discovered by some other person. "Who knows," thought he, " but this night-walking old fellow of the haunted house may be in the habit of haunting every visitor, and may give a hint to some shrewder fellow than myself, who will take a shorter

229

cut to the well than by the way of Albany? " He wished a thousand times that the babbling old ghost was laid in the Red Sea, and his rambling portrait with him. He was in a perfect fever to depart. Two or three days elapsed before any opportunity presented for returning down the river. They were ages to Dolph, notwithstanding that he was basking in the smiles of the pretty Marie, and daily getting more and more enamoured.

At length the very sloop from which he had been knocked overboard prepared to make sail. Dolph made an awkward apology to his host for his sudden departure. Antony Vander Heyden was sorely astonished. He had concerted half a dozen excursions into the wilderness; and his Indians were actually preparing for a grand expedition to one of the lakes. He took Dolph aside, and exerted his eloquence to get him to abandon all thoughts of business and to remain with him, but in vain; and he at length gave up the attempt, observing, " that it was a thousand pities so fine a young man should throw himself away." Heer Antony, however, gave him a hearty shake by the hand at parting, with a favorite fowling-piece, and an invitation to come to his house whenever he revisited Albany. The pretty little Marie said nothing; but as he gave her a farewell kiss, her dimpled cheek turned pale, and a tear stood in her eye.

Dolph sprang lightly on board of the vessel. They hoisted sail; the wind was fair; they soon lost sight of Albany, its green hills and embowered islands. They were wafted gayly past the Kaatskill Mountains, whose fairy heights were bright and cloudless. They passed prosperously through the highlands, without any molestation from the Dunderberg goblin and his crew;

they swept on across Haverstraw Bay, and by Croton Point, and through the Tappaan Zee, and under the Palisadoes, until, in the afternoon of the third day, they saw the promontory of Hoboken hanging like a cloud in the air; and, shortly after, the roofs of the Manhattoes rising out of the water.

Dolph's first care was to repair to his mother's house; for he was continually goaded by the idea of the uneasiness she must experience on his account. He was puzzling his brains, as he went along, to think how he should account for his absence without betraying the secrets of the haunted house. In the midst of these cogitations he entered the street in which his mother's house was situated, when he was thunderstruck at beholding it a heap of ruins.

There had evidently been a great fire, which had destroyed several large houses, and the humble dwelling of poor Dame Heyliger had been involved in the conflagration. The walls were not so completely destroyed but that Dolph could distinguish some traces of the scene of his childhood. The fireplace, about which he had often played, still remained, ornamented with Dutch tiles, illustrating passages in Bible history on which he had many a time gazed with admiration. Among the rubbish lay the wreck of the good dame's elbow-chair, from which she had given him so many a wholesome precept; and hard by it was the family Bible, with brass clasps, — now, alas! reduced almost to a cinder.

For a moment Dolph was overcome by this dismal sight, for he was seized with the fear that his mother had perished in the flames. He was relieved, however, from his horrible apprehension by one of the neighbors, who happened to come by and informed him that his mother was yet alive.

The good woman had, indeed, lost everything by this unlooked-for calamity; for the populace had been so intent upon saving the fine furniture of her rich neighbors, that the little tenement, and the little all of poor Dame Heyliger, had been suffered to consume without interruption; had it not been for the gallant assistance of her old crony, Peter de Groodt, the worthy dame and her cat might have shared the fate of their habitation.

As it was, she had been overcome with fright and affliction, and lay ill in body and sick at heart. The public, however, had showed her its wonted kindness. The furniture of her rich neighbors being, as far as possible, rescued from the flames; themselves duly and ceremoniously visited and condoled with on the injury of their property, and their ladies commiserated on the agitation of their nerves; the public, at length, began to recollect something about poor Dame Heyliger. She forthwith became again a subject of universal sympathy; everybody pitied her more than ever; and if pity could but have been coined into cash — good Lord! how rich she would have been!

It was now determined, in good earnest, that something ought to be done for her without delay. The Dominie, therefore, put up prayers for her on Sunday, in which all the congregation joined most heartily. Even Cobus Groesbeek, the alderman, and Mynheer Milledollar, the great Dutch merchant, stood up in their pews, and did not spare their voices on the occasion; and it was thought the prayers of such great men could not but

232

have their due weight. Doctor Knipperhausen, too, visited her professionally, and gave her abundance of advice gratis, and was universally lauded for his charity. As to her old friend, Peter de Groodt, he was a poor man, whose pity and prayers and advice could be of but little avail, so he gave her all that was in his power — he gave her shelter.

To the humble dwelling of Peter de Groodt, then, did Dolph turn his steps. On his way thither he recalled all the tenderness and kindness of his simple-hearted parent, her indulgence of his errors, her blindness to his faults; and then he bethought himself of his own idle, harum-scarum life. " I've been a sad scapegrace," said Dolph, shaking his head sorrowfully. " I've been a complete sink-pocket, that's the truth of it. But," added he briskly, and clasping his hands, " only let her live — only let her live — and I will show myself indeed a son! "

As Dolph approached the house he met Peter de Groodt coming out of it. The old man started back aghast, doubting whether it was not a ghost that stood before him. It being bright daylight, however, Peter soon plucked up heart, satisfied that no ghost dare show his face in such clear sunshine. Dolph now learned from the worthy sexton the consternation and rumor to which his mysterious disappearance had given rise. It had been universally believed that he had been spirited away by those hobgoblin gentry that infested the haunted house; and old Abraham Vandozer, who lived by the great buttonwood trees, near the three-mile stone, affirmed that he had heard a terrible noise in the air, as he was going home late at night, which seemed just as if a flock of wild geese were overhead, passing off towards the northward. The haunted house was, in consequence, looked upon with ten times more awe than ever; nobody would venture to pass a night in it for the world, and even the doctor had ceased to make his expeditions to it in the daytime.

It required some preparation before Dolph's return could be made known to his mother, the poor soul having bewailed him as lost; and her spirits having been sorely broken down by a number of comforters, who daily cheered her with stories of ghosts, and of people carried away by the devil. He found her confined to her bed, with the other member of the Heyliger family, the good dame's cat, purring beside her, but sadly singed, and utterly despoiled of those whiskers which were the glory of her physiognomy. The poor woman threw her arms about Dolph's neck. " My boy! my boy! art thou still alive? " For a time she seemed to have forgotten all her losses and troubles in her joy at his return. Even the sage grimalkin showed indubitable signs of joy at the return of the youngster. She saw, perhaps, that they were a forlorn and undone family, and felt a touch of that kindliness which fellow-sufferers only know. But, in truth, cats are a slandered people; they have more affection in them than the world commonly gives them credit for.

The good dame's eyes glistened as she saw one being at least, besides herself, rejoiced at her son's return. " Tib knows thee! poor dumb beast! " said she, smoothing down the mottled coat of her favorite; then recollecting herself, with a melancholy shake of the head, " Ah, my poor Dolph! " exclaimed she, " thy mother can help thee no longer! She can no longer help herself! What will become of thee, my poor boy! "

" Mother," said Dolph, " don't talk in that strain; I've been too long a charge upon you; it's now my part to take care of you in your old days. Come, be of good cheer! you and I and Tib will all see better days. I'm here, you see, young and sound and hearty; then don't let us despair; I dare say things will all, somehow or other, turn out for the best."

While this scene was going on with the Heyliger family, the news was carried to Doctor Knipperhausen of the safe return of his disciple. The little doctor scarce knew whether to rejoice or be sorry at the tidings. He was happy at having the foul reports which had prevailed concerning his country mansion thus disproved; but he grieved at having his disciple, of whom he had supposed himself fairly disencumbered, thus drifting back a heavy charge upon his hands. While balancing between these two feelings, he was determined by the councils of Frau Ilsy, who advised him to take advantage of the truant absence of the youngster, and shut the door upon him forever.

At the hour of bedtime, therefore, when it was supposed the recreant disciple would seek his old quarters, everything was prepared for his reception. Dolph, having talked his mother into a state of tranquillity, sought the mansion of his quondam master, and raised the knocker with a faltering hand. Scarcely, however, had it given a dubious rap, when the doctor's head, in a red nightcap, popped out of one window, and the nouse-keeper's, in a white nightcap, out of another. He was now greeted with a tremendous volley of hard names and hard language, mingled with invaluable pieces of advice, such as are seldom ventured to be given excepting to a friend in distress, or a culprit at the bar. In a few moments, not a window in the street but had its particular nightcap, listening to the shrill treble of Frau Ilsy, and the gutteral croaking of Dr. Knipperhausen; and the word went from window to window, " Ah! here's Dolph Heyliger come back, and at his old pranks again." In short, poor Dolph found he was likely to get nothing from the doctor but good advice; a commodity so abundant as even to be thrown out of the window; so he was fain to beat a retreat, and take up his quarters for the night under the lowly roof of honest Peter de Groodt.

The next morning, bright and early, Dolph was out at the haunted house. Everything looked just as he had left it. The fields were grass-grown and matted, and appeared as if nobody had traversed them since his departure. With palpitating heart he hastened to the well. He looked down into it, and saw that it was of great depth, with water at the bottom. He had provided himself with a strong line, such as the fishermen use on the banks of Newfoundland. At the end was a heavy plummet and a large fish-hook. With this he began to sound the bottom of the well, and to angle about in the water. The water was of some depth; there was also much rubbish, stones from the top having fallen in. Several times his hook got entangled, and he came near breaking his line. Now and then, too, he hauled up mere trash, such as the skull of a horse, an iron hoop, and a shattered iron-bound bucket. He had now been several hours employed without finding anything to repay his trouble, or to encourage him to proceed. He began to think himself a great fool, to be thus decoyed into a wild-goose chase by mere dreams, and was on the point of throwing line and all into the well, and giving up all further angling.

" One more cast of the line," said he, " and that shall be the last." As he sounded, he felt the plummet slip, as it were, through the interstices of loose stones; and as he drew back the line, he felt that the hook had taken hold of something heavy. He had to manage his line with great caution, lest it should be broken by the strain upon it. By degrees the rubbish which lay upon the article he had hooked gave way; he drew it to the surface of the water, and what was his rapture at seeing something like silver glittering at the end of his line! Almost breathless with anxiety, he drew it up to the mouth of the well, surprised at its great weight, and fearing every instant that his hook would slip from its hold, and his prize tumble again to the bottom. At length he landed it safe beside the well. It was a great silver porringer, of an ancient form, richly embossed, and with armorial bearings engraved on its side, similar to those over his mother's mantelpiece. The lid was fastened on by several twists of wire; Dolph loosened them with a trembling hand and, on lifting the lid, behold! the vessel was filled with broad golden pieces, of a coinage which he had never seen before! It was evident he had lit on the place where Killian Vander Spiegel had concealed his treasure.

Fearful of being seen by some straggler, he cautiously retired, and buried his pot of money in a secret place. He now

237

spread terrible stories about the haunted house, and deterred
every one from approaching it, while he made frequent visits
to it in stormy days, when no one was stirring in the neighboring
fields; though, to tell the truth, he did not care to venture there
in the dark. For once in his life he was diligent and industrious,
and followed up his new trade of angling with such persever-
ance and success, that in a little while he had hooked up wealth
enough to make him, in those modern days, a rich burgher
for life.

It would be tedious to detail minutely the rest of this story.
To tell how he gradually managed to bring his property into
use without exciting surprise and inquiry, — how he satisfied
all scruples with regard to retaining the property, and at the
same time gratified his own feelings by marrying the pretty
Marie Vander Heyden, — and how he and Heer Antony had
many a merry and roving expedition together.

Dolph took his mother home to live with him, and cherished

her in her old days. The good dame, too, had the satisfaction of no longer hearing her son made the theme of censure; on the contrary, he grew daily in public esteem; everybody spoke well of him and his wines and the lordliest burgomaster was never known to decline his invitation to dinner. Dolph often related, at his own table, the wicked pranks which had once been the abhorrence of the town; but they were now considered excellent jokes, and the gravest dignitary was fain to hold his sides when listening to them. No one was more struck with Dolph's increasing merit than his old master the doctor; and so forgiving was Dolph, that he absolutely employed the doctor as his family physician, only taking care that his prescriptions should be always thrown out of the window. His mother had often her junto of old cronies to take a snug cup of tea with her in her comfortable little parlor; and Peter de Groodt, as he sat by the fireside, with one of her grandchildren on his knee, would many a time congratulate her upon her son turning out so great a man; upon which the good old soul would wag her head with exultation, and exclaim: " Ah, neighbor, neighbor! did I not say that Dolph would one day or other hold up his head with the best of them? "

Thus did Dolph Heyliger go on, cheerily and prosperously, growing merrier as he grew older and wiser, and completely falsifying the old proverb about money got over the devil's back; for he made good use of his wealth, and became a distinguished citizen, and a valuable member of the community. He was a great promoter of public institutions, such as beefsteak societies and catch-clubs. He presided at all public dinners, and was the first that introduced turtle from the West Indies. He improved the breed of race-horses and game cocks, and was so great a patron of modest merit, that any one who could sing a good song, or tell a good story, was sure to find a place at his table.

He was a member, too, of the corporation, made several laws for the protection of game and oysters, and bequeathed to the board a large silver punch-bowl, made out of the identical porringer before mentioned, and which is in the possession of the corporation to this very day.

Finally, he died, in a florid old age, of an apoplexy at a corporation feast, and was buried with great honors in the yard of the little Dutch church in Garden Street, where his tombstone may still be seen with a modest epitaph in Dutch, by his friend Mynheer Justus Benson, an ancient and excellent poet of the province.

In addition to his other accomplishments, Dolph Heyliger was noted for being the ablest drawer of the long-bow in the whole province.